Stacey's Big Crush

**Other books by
Ann M. Martin**

Rachel Parker, Kindergarten Show-off

Eleven Kids, One Summer

Ma and Pa Dracula

Yours Turly, Shirley

Ten Kids, No Pets

Slam Book

Just a Summer Romance

Missing Since Monday

With You and Without You

Me and Katie (the Pest)

Stage Fright

Inside Out

Bummer Summer

BABY-SITTERS LITTLE SISTER series

THE BABY-SITTERS CLUB mysteries

(see back of the book for a more complete listing)

THE BABY-SITTERS CLUB series

Stacey's Big Crush
Ann M. Martin

AN
APPLE
PAPERBACK

SCHOLASTIC INC.
New York Toronto London Auckland Sydney

Special thanks to Nicholas Lerangis
for his rendition of
"The Three Billy Goats Gruff"

Cover art by Hodges Soileau

ISBN 0-590-45667-9

12 11 10 9 8 7 6 5 4 3 2 1   3 4 5 6 7 8/9

Printed in the U.S.A.   40

First Scholastic printing, June 1993

The author gratefully acknowledges
Peter Lerangis
for his help in
preparing this manuscript.

Stacey's Big Crush

CHAPTER 1

I love the smell of lilacs.

"If x = 4 . . ."

But there should be a law against growing them too near a school.

" . . . and 3x + 9 = y . . ."

Especially near a math class with open windows. Like *my* math class.

" . . . then find the value of . . ."

I knew Mr. Zizmore was giving an oral problem. Usually I pay very close attention. In fact, I adore math. Really. But with the breeze blowing in, and that incredible smell, I was feeling distracted.

"Stacey?"

Oops. Mr. Zizmore was calling on me. I had no idea what he'd just said. I looked down at my notebook, hoping for a clue. I felt like a fool.

"Um . . . find the value of what?" I asked.

"Y."

"Y?"

Irv Hirsch said "Why not?" in the back of the room, and half the class broke out in giggles.

Mr. Z. shook his head. "Stacey McGill, when *you* start drifting away, I know it must be spring."

I heard a few more snickers. I was embarrassed. But in a way, Mr. Z. was complimenting me. He knows math is my favorite subject, and he knows only something extreme (like lilacs) would draw my attention away.

Actually, lilacs are pretty exotic to me. Where I come from, New York City, there aren't any. Well, there *are*, but they're in buckets of water at corner markets, and they've been picked already so the aroma is almost gone. I do miss a lot of things about New York, but Stoneybrook definitely smells better at this time of year. How do you know it's a spring day in New York City?

1. By touching the radiator to see if the super has turned off the heat.

2. By listening to the weather report.

3. By looking out the window to see what people are wearing. (This choice only applies if you have an apartment facing the street.)

Can you tell I'm a real New Yorker? I am. I was born there. I'm an only child, and my parents took me everywhere — shows, restaurants, museums, concerts, festivals, you name it. So I'm really comfortable in the city, despite the grime and crime and other bad stuff. But around the time I started seventh grade, my dad's company transferred him to Stoneybrook. So it was Bye-Bye Big Apple.

To me, Stoneybrook was "the country." Actually, it's a small town in Connecticut, but it's awfully cozy and quiet compared to NYC. It's also the home of my best friends and the Baby-sitters Club (which I'll tell you about later).

Now I'm thirteen and in eighth grade at Stoneybrook Middle School. But I haven't been in Stoneybrook the whole time. For a while last year we moved to New York again, when Dad's company transferred him back. By that time I'd adjusted and made my new friends *here*. Leaving them was sad. But it was fun to see my old neighborhood (in a new apartment) and my old friends.

Well, the fun didn't last long. My parents had been getting on each other's nerves for awhile. Soon they were arguing all the time. Then the fights became long shouting matches. Before I knew it, they sprang the bad news on me. They were getting a divorce.

I was kind of expecting it, but it still shocked me. Here was the worst part: Dad decided to stay in New York, but Mom wanted to go back to Stoneybrook. And they asked me to choose which place I wanted to live in! It was, like, "Do you want to be with *me* or not?" I was afraid to decide on either place. After a long time (and a lot of crying) we finally made a deal. I would live with my mom in Stoney-brook — but I had to be allowed to make lots of visits to New York! (It's only a train ride away.)

So here I am. Mom and I live in a nice, small house. The divorce seems to be working out all right, I guess. (Well, at least they're not slugging it out.) Dad sends his alimony and child care payments regularly (yea, Dad!) but Mom decided to supplement them by taking a job as a buyer at Bellair's Department Store (yea, Mom!).

So I guess that makes me a Divorced Kid and a Latchkey Kid. I don't mind the Latchkey part. It's the Divorced part that's hard. For a long time, I felt as if I had to be Super Daugh-ter. I thought I needed to please both parents all the time. And my parents weren't making things easy for me, either. Each of them always grilled me about the other, as if they were arguing *through* me. Finally everything came to a head. It started when my mom got really sick recently. She was laid up in bed on the night I was supposed to go to an important dinner for my dad in New York. I tried to be my mom's nursemaid *and* make the trip. Well, everything got botched up. I overscheduled mom's caretakers. I cut my NYC trip short, which made Dad angry. I ended up exhausting myself.

So I did some thinking. I realized I'd been trying way too hard. I had a long talk with my mom. She told me I should learn to take care of myself first, which was a good idea. Since then I've been trying to follow that advice.

Funny how divorce complicates everything.

Okay. I got off track. Where was I? Oh, yes, lilacs and pre-algebra. That fateful May morning in Mr. Zizmore's class.

Why do I say fateful? You'll find out.

Mr. Z. repeated the problem. I scribbled furiously in my notebook. "Twenty-one!"

"Good recovery," Mr. Z. said, smiling.

I heard a loud yawn behind me. Mr. Z. gave Peter Hayes a withering glance (Don't you love that expression? I read it in a book once). "Mister Hayes, I'm so sorry these problems are too rudimentary for your keen quantitative capabilities. Here's one for you to solve . . ."

Some people yell when they get fed up. Mr. Z. just uses more syllables. Poor Peter. Mr. Z.

gave him the toughest problem he could think of. Peter squirmed and tried not to look humiliated.

I guess Mr. Z. began feeling sorry for him, because he said, "I guess this is just one of those days, huh? I have to admit, I have trouble concentrating when the temperature gets above sixty-five, myself."

You could practically hear the entire class sigh with relief. Mr. Z., when you get right down to it, is pretty cool. He's patient and friendly — and he makes math come alive, which is not an easy thing to do.

(Besides, he tells me I'm his star student, which makes me feel great.)

So you can imagine how I felt when he made the next announcement.

"Okay, I'm going to knock off a little early," he said, looking at the clock, "because I have something to tell you. Tomorrow's going to be the last day I'll be teaching this class."

We looked at him curiously.

"As part of the master's program at Stoneybrook Community College," he went on, "a student teacher will be taking over the class for the last month."

Most of the class groaned with disappointment. I could tell Mr. Z. didn't expect that reaction. He had to force back a smile.

"I'm going to miss you, too," he said. "But

I'll be back to administer your final exam. I'll also drop into class from time to time to supervise — "

"Us or her?" someone called out.

Mr. Z. chuckled. "Uh, *both*, after hearing that comment. And it's a him, not a her. His name is Mr. Ellenburg, and I expect you not to give him a hard time. These weeks are crucial. Mr. Ellenburg will finish the last unit and prepare you for the final."

Mr. Ellenburg? Already I didn't like him. That name made me think of a nerd with no sense of humor.

(That was unfair, I know. When I first heard the name *Zizmore*, I thought of someone with a horrible acne problem. Like *Zits more*. The thought still embarrasses me.)

The bell rang. I let out a sigh.

As I picked up my books and started to walk out, Mr. Z. smiled at me. "Don't look so blue," he said. "I'm sure you'll continue to do just great, Stacey. And besides, Wesley Ellenburg is a very talented teacher. I've interviewed him."

"Thanks," I said. "Okay. See you tomorrow."

"You bet."

Mr. Z. was nice to reassure me. But he sort of missed the point. I wasn't super worried about not doing well. It was just going to be hard to lose my favorite teacher, that's all.

Besides, the kids in class have never been kind to substitutes. The last sub was a disaster. One kid, Irv, spent the period speaking with this strange foreign accent. The poor sub would answer him with slow, exaggerated sentences. (She thought the class was laughing at Irv, not her.) And each time she turned her back, Peter Hayes would toss a ballpoint pen up to the ceiling, trying to get it to stick in the acoustical tile. By the end of the period, three pens were hanging like stalactites. When the bell rang, Pete calmly stood on his desk and pulled them out, while Irv walked out with a smile, saying, "Thank you, I thoroughly enjoyed that lesson," in perfect English.

But I didn't tell Mr. Z. any of that. I figured I'd just be brave and face the next few weeks with Mr. Ellenburg.

Mr. *Wesley* Ellenburg.

I was already feeling sorry for the guy.

And for myself.

Math is my last class of the day, so I went straight to my locker. I pulled out the books I'd need for homework, slammed the door shut, and walked to the school entrance.

Claudia Kishi was waiting there. She's my best friend. (I used to have another best friend, Laine Cummings, who lives in New York. But we had a huge fight because she was so mean to my Stoneybrook friends — so Claud is now my one-and-only-best.)

"Hi, Stacey," Claudia said.

"Hi."

Claudia immediately looked concerned. "Is something wrong?"

I explained what had happened in math class. Claudia nodded and listened, but I could tell my problem sounded a little strange to her. "Either way," she said with a shrug, "you still end up having to learn math."

To Claudia, taking math is like taking medicine. You do it only as long as you have to, and *how* you do it doesn't matter much.

The door opened and Dawn Schafer walked out with Mary Anne Spier. "Stacey's totally bummed," Claudia said with a grim look. "Her math teacher's leaving."

"Oh," Dawn said blankly.

"Too bad," Mary Anne added.

"The new one's named Wesley Baconburger," Claudia went on.

"*Clau-aud.*" I couldn't help giggling. I could tell I was going to get no sympathy. "It's Ellenburg."

"Who's Ellen Burg?"

That was Kristy Thomas's voice. She'd just come through the door, followed by Jessi Ramsey and Mallory Pike.

"Stacey's new math teacher," Claudia replied.

"Do you like her?" Mallory asked.

"No — it's a *he*," I protested.

"A guy named Ellen?" Jessi said.

"I don't believe this!" I threw up my hands. "Claudia, this is your fault."

Claudia laughed. The others looked at us as if we'd lost our minds. ("The others," by the way, are the other regular members of the Baby-sitters Club, or BSC. The seven of us often meet after school, even though we sometimes have an *official* meeting later on.) Claud repeated what I'd told her about math class, only this time she got the details right.

Fortunately we didn't have to dwell on the subject. We were saved by the bus — Kristy's bus, that is. Kristy's the only one of us who lives too far from school to walk home.

"You'll survive, Stace," Kristy called over her shoulder as she ran to the bus. "See you at five-thirty! 'Bye!"

" 'Bye!" we called back.

(Five-thirty, in case you're wondering, is the meeting time for the BSC.)

The rest of us stayed and gabbed for a while about the Spring Dance that was coming up at the end of the month. Soon Jessi had to leave for a sitting job, and Mallory had to go to an orthodontist appointment.

10

Mary Anne, Dawn, Claudia, and I walked home together. We passed *many* lilac bushes. At each one we took deep breaths and smiled.

By the time I got home, the lilacs had taken effect. Not to mention the warm sunshine and the clear, cool breeze. I felt so *romantic*. Mary Anne had gone to her boyfriend's house, and I found myself wishing I were in her shoes. Not that I had her boyfriend. Just *a* boyfriend. (What is it about the spring?)

Don't get the wrong impression. It isn't that I've never gone out with guys. I have. And technically, Sam Thomas (Kristy's older brother) and I *are* going out. Well, sort of. I mean, he isn't my boyfriend but he isn't exactly *not* my boyfriend. We *like* each other a lot, but it isn't LOVE or anything. Besides, we'd kind of drifted apart in recent weeks. Sigh.

I used my key to open the front door. It still felt a little funny walking into an empty house. I went straight to the phone. I thought about calling Sam, but instead I called my mom.

"Bellair's," her voice said.

"Hi, it's me," I replied.

"Hi, honey! How are you?"

"Okay. How's work?"

"Busy. All kinds of reorders on swimwear already. Listen, sweetheart, I have a client on the other line. Can I call you back?"

"Sure," I said. " 'Bye."

" 'Bye."

I walked to the fridge, feeling kind of glum and lonely. I pulled out some cottage cheese and a peach. Secretly I wished I could pig out on some chocolate. But only for a moment. For me, chocolate is out of the question. No, I'm not on a diet. Well, I *am*, but I'm on it for life. See, I have diabetes, which means my body can't properly regulate the sugar in my blood. I have to inject myself every day with insulin. (It sounds gross, I know, but I have no choice.) The insulin helps break down the sugar into stuff your body needs, like protein, energy, and fat. In nondiabetics, the pancreas makes insulin naturally — and in the right amounts. We diabetics have to constantly test our blood for insulin levels. Too much insulin is almost as bad as too little. You can go into something called insulin shock. When I feel *that* happening, I have to gobble a candy bar or a spoonful of honey right away.

I ate my snack. Then I trudged off to my room to do homework. Ah, poor me. Boy-friendless and momless, on a beautiful after-noon. But I knew my lonely feeling wouldn't last long. In an hour and a half, I'd be at Claudia's house for a Monday meeting of the Baby-sitters Club.

CHAPTER 2

Crunch. Claudia pulled a plastic bag from behind her pillow. "These were on sale at the health food store."

She held the bag out to me.

"All-natural Crispy Rancho-style Veggie-Rice Nuggets with Nacho Substitute Cheese-food Flavor?" I said, reading the label.

"That's a mouthful," Mallory remarked, biting into a Kit Kat.

Kristy made a face. "They look like moldy Cheez Doodles. No wonder they were on sale."

I opened the bag and ate a nugget. "Well, they taste great."

Dawn reached over and took one, too. "Yum. You ought to try one, Kristy."

"No, thanks, it has substitute cheese," Kristy said with a sneer. "I prefer something *pure.*"

"Have a Mallomar," Claudia offered, holding out an open box.

"Sure!" Kristy grabbed two.

Dawn groaned. "That's pure?"

"Yes, these are made with organic . . . marshmallow," Claudia said with a straight face.

Dawn laughed so hard she almost sprayed her nuggets across the room. (Dawn is a real health food nut.)

"Hi!" Jessi called out as she walked into Claudia's bedroom. "Did I miss something funny?"

"Today we're only having health food snacks," Claudia said.

"Yeah, Organic Mallomars or Mildew Munchies," Kristy mumbled between bites.

This time we all started giggling.

Jessi smiled. "Spring fever hits the Baby-sitters Club!" she said, sitting on the floor.

Jessi was right. We were feeling a little silly. Which was fine. One of the things I like best about the BSC is that we can just relax and be ourselves.

Okay, I promised I'd tell about the Baby-sitters Club, so here goes. You already know we're best friends, but our main purpose is to get baby-sitting jobs. (Surprised?) We meet at Claud's house from 5:30 to 6:00 on Mondays, Wednesdays, and Fridays. We chose Claud's because she's the only one of us who has a private phone. For the BSC, a phone is an absolute necessity. Neighborhood parents call during meeting times to line up sitters. Since there are seven of us (nine, if you count our associate members, Shannon Kilbourne and Logan Bruno), we manage to fill almost every request.

How do parents know about us? We advertise. We hand out fliers and we put up signs on supermarket bulletin boards. But our best advertisements are happy clients. They become regulars, and they spread the word about us.

It's a great idea — for us and for parents. *We* get to have fun, make some money, and spend time with kids. And *they* can line up an experienced, reliable sitter with just one call.

We started the club in seventh grade, when Kristy Thomas had a brainstorm. Way back then, in the year 1 BBSC (Before Baby-sitters Club), Mrs. Thomas was frantically trying to line up a sitter for Kristy's younger brother, David Michael. She made a zillion calls before she got someone. Kristy put her brain to work — and *voilà!* She had a revolutionary idea. Why not have one central number for sitters, like a service?

Kristy, Claudia Kishi, Mary Anne Spier and I were the charter members, but we quickly grew. Now we've become a successful business. Yes, business. We have officers, rules, record-keeping, and dues.

And food. As you probably guessed, eating is a big part of BSC meetings. But let me set the record straight. It's not *all* we do. Far from it. It's just that Claudia has this thing about junk food. She collects it. Claud's room is a Junk-Food Treasure Island. If you tried to "mark the spot," though, you'd have to put X's everywhere. Since her parents are anti-junk food, Claud finds all kinds of interesting hiding places for her loot — under pillows, behind books, inside shoe boxes, between mattresses. (She also hides Nancy Drew books. She loves them, but her parents think she should only read "literature.") The minute a meeting starts, out comes the food. Claud is very generous with it, and she even makes sure to have healthy or sugarless snacks for Dawn and me.

How would you picture a person who is obsessed with Ring-Dings, Snickers, Twinkies, Milky Ways, and Yankee Doodles? Well, guess again. Claudia is as trim as a model, and she has perfect skin. She is gorgeous, too, with long, silky black hair and almond eyes (she's Japanese-American). She's also one of the two fashion plates of the BSC. The other? Hrrrmph. Yours truly. Okay, I know it sounds

16

snobbish, but all I'm saying is that Claud and I are the most clothes-crazy of the members. We like to follow new trends (and set them, if we can). Claudia likes experimenting more than I do, though. She can throw together the wildest hats and vests and shoes — stuff you wouldn't dream of wearing — and look sensational. She loves to wear her hair in different ways and is crazy about wild-colored barrettes.

Creativity just spills out of Claudia. You would not believe her artwork. She can paint, sculpt, draw, and make jewelry. Once she had an art show in her garage. The show was called "Disposable Comestibles," and it was all paintings and drawings of . . . junk food! Oh, that title was not Claud's idea. Her older sister, Janine, thought of it. Janine is into big words — and Calculus and Advanced Everything. She has an IQ of 196, and she takes courses at Stoneybrook Community College (maybe with Wesley Ellenburg). Claudia, on the other hand, is not a good student. (Her spelling is atrocious.) For a long time she felt her parents favored Janine, but lately they've begun to realize how special Claudia's talents are.

Another thing. Claud is our vice-president, mainly because we use her room for headquarters. Plus sometimes she has to take calls from parents who forget our official hours.

Our president is our founder, Kristy Thomas. She was born for the job. She's loud and bossy (but we love her anyway). And she's always full of ideas. Without Kristy, we'd probably be a lot less organized and efficient.

Kristy's mind is amazing. She tries to solve problems before they happen. Here's an example. Not long after she started the BSC, she figured out a potential *disadvantage* of our club. Clients would not be guaranteed the same sitter each time. Parents would have to repeat instructions to each new sitter. Then the sitter and the kids would have to get acquainted from scratch. So Kristy dreamt up the BSC notebook. In it, we write down a summary of each job — special instructions, the kids' needs and preferences, funny stories, *anything*. Kristy insists that we write in the notebook after each job, even if nothing much has happened. That can be a bit of a pain. But all of us agree that the book is a huge help.

Kristy also invented the BSC record book. That's where we keep a schedule of our jobs, plus a client list — including addresses, phone numbers, the rates they pay, and their kids' names and ages.

Another brilliant Kristy idea was Kid-Kits. They're just cardboard boxes filled with simple toys, games, and books — mostly art supplies and stuff we scrounge from our houses. What kid would want to play with old junk like that? You'd be surprised. Our charges *adore* Kid-Kits.

Then there's Kristy's Krushers, a softball team she organized for kids who weren't ready for Little League. Kristy, by the way, is great at sports. She's small and compact, and she usually wears sweats or jeans and a T-shirt or a turtleneck. She never wears makeup, though, and doesn't do much with her long brown hair.

Kristy is so down-to-earth, you'd never guess her stepdad was the richest man in Stoneybrook. Well, maybe that's an exaggeration, but he's definitely well-off. Which is great, because most of Kristy's life hasn't been so privileged. She used to live in a small house across the street from Claudia's. Not long after David Michael was born, about seven years ago, Kristy's dad just left the family. No explanation, no nothing. He hardly ever calls his kids, so he's *persona non grata* around here. (My mom uses that expression. It means "person not wanted.") Mrs. Thomas held down a job and raised Kristy and her three brothers by herself. Then one day she fell in love with Watson Brewer. He's a really sweet guy, very quiet, and a terrific gardener. Well, he and Mrs. Thomas got married and the Thomases moved in with the Brewers (Watson has two kids from *his* previous marriage, who live in his house on alternate weekends and holidays). The family has grown to include Emily Michelle, an adopted Vietnamese girl, and Kristy's grandmother, Nannie. *And* they have all kinds of pets. So the Brewer house is a pretty busy place, but there's lots of room. It's an enormous old mansion, *way* on the other side of town. Kristy has to be driven to and from BSC meetings (usually by her oldest brother Charlie).

"Hrr-rmm, hrr-rrmm." Kristy cleared her throat. Claudia's digital clock read 5:29. I was sitting in my usual position, cross-legged on the bed, sandwiched between Mary Anne and Claudia. Jessi and Mal were on the floor. Dawn was sitting backward on Claudia's desk chair.

Kristy was perched on a canvas director's chair, wearing her trusty visor. As always, she had one eye on the clock. The moment it hit 5:30, she blurted out, "This meeting will come to order!"

We all sat up a little straighter, waiting for Kristy's next line (which is "Any new business?").

"Any new business?" (See, she never lets us down.)

"Dues day!" I said. I am the club treasurer, the one who has to take a share of everyone's

20

hard-earned money on Mondays. We use the money to pay Charlie Thomas for his gas expenses, to help Claudia with her phone bill, and to buy new things for Kid-Kits. If any money is left over, we sometimes plan a pizza party or something.

My position, of course, is the most beloved of all. You can tell from the reactions:

"Already?"

"Do we have to?"

"Ugggh, that's right . . ."

"Can't we skip this week?"

I did my duty and collected the money. (The grumbling is sort of a tradition. My friends don't really mean what they say. At least I hope they don't.)

No sooner did the last coin jingle into our treasury (an old manila envelope) then the phone rang.

"Baby-sitters Club," Claudia said into the receiver. "Oh, hi, Mrs. Barrett. . . . Next Tuesday? Oh . . . okay, I'll check and call you right back. . . . 'Bye." She hung up and turned to Mary Anne. "The Barrett kids, two weeks from tomorrow?"

"Um, let me check," Mary Anne said.

Mary Anne is our secretary. She handles the record book. Talk about a complicated job. She has to keep our client list up-to-date, keep track of our schedules (Jessi's ballet classes,

Mal's orthodontist appointments, Kristy's Krushers practices, Claud's art classes), schedule our jobs, *and* try to make sure each of us has a roughly equal amount of work. Needless to say, Mary Anne is very organized. Plus she has the world's neatest handwriting.

Personality-wise, Mary Anne is the exact opposite of Kristy. She's shy and quiet, she hates anything athletic, and she's *very* sensitive. I think the supermarket stocks extra Kleenex boxes when the Spier family goes shopping. I have seen Mary Anne cry at the sight of a limping squirrel. Her boyfriend jokes about having to take out flood insurance after they watched a tape of *Love Story* together.

Guess who's best friends with shy, retiring Mary Anne? Loud, unretiring Kristy. Go figure. (I love that expression. The newspaperstand guy on my dad's block in New York says it all the time. My dad will remark about something unusual, like, "Can you believe this, ninety degrees in April?" The guy will shake his head and answer, "Go figure.") Another interesting thing about Mary Anne is this: of all the BSC members, she's the only one with a steady boyfriend. His name's Logan Bruno (yes, the same Logan Bruno who's an associate BSC member). He's handsome and outgoing and very athletic. They've had their ups and downs, but lately they seem very close.

Mary Anne's also in eighth grade, but when I first met her, I thought she was a year or two younger than me. Her hair was in pigtails and she wore little-girl dresses. At that time, she lived alone with her dad (her mom died when Mary Anne was a baby). Mr. Spier's a nice man, but he was incredibly strict, with all kinds of rules and curfews. Luckily, all that has changed. Mary Anne has been set free! She wears tasteful, stylish clothes and recently got her hair cut in a short new style. Why? Because her dad got remarried and loosened up. The woman who helped change his life (and Mary Anne's) was none other than . . .

Dawn Schafer's mom! Yes, they're married. But before I tell you that saga, let me tell you about Dawn. Like me, she's an import — meaning she came to Stoneybrook from afar. *Really* afar. She moved here with her mom and brother Jeff from sunny, beach-covered southern California, after her parents divorced. Dawn's hair is light blonde (almost white) and she always has this healthy glow. (If you met her, you'd see right away why her parents called her "Dawn.") Like me, Dawn eats no sweets. But she goes much further. She doesn't eat red meat either, and she prefers organically grown food, and stuff like tofu and alfalfa sprouts. No, she's not a diabetic — she *likes* to eat that way.

Go figure.

Anyway, Mrs. Schafer grew up in Stoneybrook. It turns out she used to date Mary Anne's dad. Well, they got together again after all those years and before we knew it, they were engaged. So now they all live in the Schafers' rambling old farmhouse (except for Jeff, who went back to California to live with his dad). And that's how Mary Anne and Dawn became stepsisters.

Dawn's our alternate officer, which means she takes over for anyone who can't make meetings. I think she's done each job at least once. She became treasurer when I moved back to New York (and she was thrilled to give me the job again when I returned).

Jessica Ramsey and Mallory Pike are our junior officers. "Junior" because they're two years younger than the rest of us. They're eleven years old and in sixth grade. They both have early curfews, so they mostly do after-school and weekend day jobs. That works out great, because it frees the rest of us for late sitting.

Mal and Jessi are best friends. They're excellent sitters, too. Each of them is the oldest kid in her family, which means each has had lots of training. Especially Mallory. She has *seven* brothers and sisters (including triplets). Jessi has two, a sister and a brother.

You already know we have a great artist in our midst, but we also have a great writer and a great ballerina. Jessi's the ballerina. She looks it, too, with long legs and perfect posture and hair always pulled back from her face. She's already danced lead roles in school productions. Mal not only writes wonderful stories, but illustrates them, too. She wants to do that for a living someday.

Jessi and Mal both love to read, and they both complain that their parents treat them like babies. (Although there has been some progress. They were allowed to get their ears pierced recently.) Physically, they couldn't be more different. Mal has pale, freckly skin, blue eyes, and frizzy reddish hair. She also wears glasses and braces (the clear kind). Jessi's skin is chocolately brown, and she has big dark eyes.

Last but not least, our associate members. I've told you a little about Logan. He loves to baby-sit, but he's usually involved in some after-school sport, so he can't be a regular member. Logan has been bitten by the cute bug (definition: major hunk). Shannon Kilbourne, our other associate member, goes to a private school called Stoneybrook Day

School. Lately she's been coming to meetings a lot. (That Monday, though, she had a drama club meeting after school.)

Okay. That covers us all. Now back to the meeting.

There we were, munching away. The Veggie-Rice Nuggets were beginning to lose their appeal. I think Claudia could sense that, because she fished out a bag of pretzels from her sock drawer. But she had to put it down on the dresser when the phone rang.

Claud chirped, "Hello, Baby-sitters Club," into the phone. "Oh, hi, Dr. Johanssen. . . . Oh, that's okay, don't worry. Let me ask." She covered the receiver and said, "Charlotte on Wednesday evening?"

Mary Anne checked the schedule and replied, "Stacey's free."

Claudia looked at me and I nodded. "Hi, it's me again," Claud said to Dr. Johanssen. "Stace will be there. . . . You're welcome. 'Bye."

Now, BSC members don't usually "reserve" their charges, but Charlotte Johanssen is a special case. She and I have become very close, almost like sisters. So no one minds if I'm given first choice to sit for Char.

Well, the week wasn't turning out badly after all. True, my favorite class was about to be taken over by some inexperienced dweeb. But the weather was nice, Claud had discovered a good new sugarless snack for me, and I was going to see my number one sitting charge in two days. It could have been worse.

CHAPTER 3

Sniff. Sniff. Sniff.

Ah, spring. The next day, Tuesday, was perfect, like the day before. Mary Anne, Dawn, and I walked home from school together *very* slowly. Spring fever slowly. I was carrying a light load, because Mr. Zizmore hadn't given us a homework assignment. I guess that was the one nice thing about having a new teacher the next day.

The rest of the BSCers were busy. Jessi had gone off to ballet. Mal and Claudia had sitting jobs. Kristy had called a Krushers practice.

As we turned onto Burnt Hill Road, Mary Anne asked, "What are you doing this afternoon?"

"The usual," I replied. "Fixing myself some cottage cheese and doing some homework."

"Sounds exciting," Dawn said.

"Want to come over?" Mary Anne suggested.

"Sure!" It was a perfect idea. I didn't feel like going home to an empty house, anyway.

Dawn and Mary Anne's house is on Burnt Hill, just past the intersection with my street. And it is *the* coolest house in Stoneybrook. Yes, even cooler than the Brewer mansion. It's this old, *old* farmhouse. It was built in the late 1700s, complete with a barn out back. Here's the best part about it: A secret passageway leads from the barn to . . . Dawn's bedroom! According to legend, the house was part of the Underground Railroad. African-American slaves would stop there on their flight away from the South.

The house looks big, but it doesn't feel that way inside. That's because the rooms are pretty small and the doorways are low. (People must have been *tiny* in the 1700s — probably because they didn't have Veggie-Rice Nuggets.)

"Hi, girls!" Mrs. Schafer called from upstairs as we walked in. She came clomping down the old wooden staircase into the living room. I could tell she'd had a haircut, because the curls in her blonde hair were tighter and bouncier than usual. "Stacey, nice to see you!"

"Nice to see you, too," I said.

"You make yourselves at home," Mrs. Schafer went on, looking suddenly distracted. "I was going to go shopping, but I can't find

29

my keys." She walked into the kitchen, muttering, "I was in here, checking to see what we need — "

Dawn followed her. She went straight to the fridge, opened it, and — *jingle, jingle* — guess what she found?

In case you haven't noticed, Mrs. Schafer is a little on the scatterbrained side. Dawn has developed a sixth sense about where her mom has forgotten things.

After we said good-bye to Mrs. Schafer, Mary Anne and Dawn scrounged up a snack from the fridge — scarves and loose change (just kidding).

We wandered out to the backyard, which is huge. Mary Anne's kitten, Tigger, followed us. As we sat on some lawn chairs, Tiggy began putting on a show. He lunged forward. He batted invisible things with his paws. He rolled around. He ran off as if he were being chased.

After a while, we were giggling uncontrollably. "Tiggy, what's gotten into you?" Mary Anne called out.

"Spring feeee-verrr . . ." Dawn said.

Soon we heard another laughing voice. We turned to see a salt-and-pepper-haired woman walking toward us.

"He's adorable!" she said.

"Oh, hi, Mrs. Stone," Dawn replied. "This

is our friend, Stacey McGill. Let me get you a chair."

"Hi, Stacey," Mrs. Stone said, shaking my hand. "Please, don't bother, Dawn. I can't stay long. I just came over to ask you girls if you could do me a favor."

"Sure," Mary Anne piped up.

Mrs. Stone laughed. "Well, don't say yes until I tell you what it is. My husband and I are going out of town on Saturday for three weeks — "

Dawn's eyes lit up. "You need someone to look after your farm?"

"Well, not exactly," Mrs. Stone replied. "We've hired someone to stop by twice a day. My main concern is leaving Elvira. She's only two months old, you know, and we've never been away from her."

"Oh," Mary Anne said, nodding solemnly.

Elvira? She named her baby Elvira, and now she was leaving the poor kid for three weeks? I felt sorry for the little girl. Well, at least her last name wasn't Ellenburg.

"You see, she has required so much extra care," Mrs. Stone went on, "what with her mother dying during the birth, poor thing. Harold and I have had to raise her ourselves, and she depends on us."

"Is she all right?" Dawn asked. She and Mary Anne seemed to know this girl, but I

31

didn't remember them talking about her.

"Oh, yes, she's quite healthy, but I don't dare leave her alone. You wouldn't believe the things she'll eat if she's not supervised. She especially likes the kitchen trash and the mail. And I just don't trust the animals with her. I'm afraid one of the horses will get annoyed and kick her."

My jaw dropped so fast I thought I'd pulled a muscle.

"Would you girls consider looking after her?" Mrs. Stone continued. "She adjusts beautifully to new people, and she's no bother at all. I'd pay you, naturally. And I could bring her over here. You could keep her in the barn."

Whaaaat? My lord! This was absolutely amazing. As I stared in disbelief, I could see Dawn looking wary. "Mrs. Stone," she said, "does Elvira have . . . horns?"

"Uh, wait a minute," I interrupted. "Just exactly who or what is Elvira?"

"Oh, I'm sorry," Mrs. Stone said cheerily. "She's a kid."

My heart sank.

"A baby goat," she added.

"Ohhh!" I said. I nodded knowingly. I tried to look as if I had known all along that Elvira was an animal.

There was no *way*, no way on Earth, that

anyone would ever know what I had been thinking.

"I think it would be fun," Mary Anne said.

"Can we see her?" Dawn asked.

"Sure!" Mrs. Stone replied. "You can come over now if you want."

So that was how we met Elvira. The Stones' farm was a long walk away, near the cemetery on the outskirts of town. (See what I meant when I said Stoneybrook was the country? Where the Stones live is pretty rural.) The farm was not exactly huge, not like farms in the movies, with crops as far as the eye can see. But I was impressed. The Stones had an awesome vegetable garden and a barn that was much bigger than Dawn's. A rusty tractor was parked near the barn, and some chickens were strutting around it, giving us the eye.

"I love this place," Dawn said.

"You've been here before?" I asked.

"Just driving by," Dawn replied. "But Mom and Richard have always been pretty friendly with the Stones."

Mrs. Stone was walking briskly ahead of us, practically sprinting. She seemed older than my parents, but life on the farm must have given her incredible stamina. "We have horses, pigs, chickens, and a couple of cows," she said over her shoulder. "It's not much, but we sure enjoy them."

We followed her into the barn. She leaned down into a small pen surrounded by a wire fence.

When she turned around, she was holding Elvira.

Elvira was all eyes and bony joints. She stared up at us, jerking her head from face to face. Beneath her chin was a thin, pointy beard. Her fur was a mottled gray-white-black, and it looked scraggly and dusty.

In other words, she was absolutely beautiful.

"Beeeaaaaahh," Elvira bleated in a tiny voice.

"Ohhhhhhhh." We all said the same thing at once. We couldn't help it. Elvira was so fragile and sweet. She had instantly stolen our hearts.

"It's okay, baby," Mrs. Stone reassured her. "She's a little nervous," she said to us. "But she'll get over it."

She put Elvira down, next to an old tennis ball. Elvira glanced at us, then skittered away on her thin, wobbly legs. When she turned around, she lowered her head and sprinted toward the ball. She butted it, and as it bounced away she looked up. We applauded wildly.

Elvira baahed again. Her lips were turned

up naturally, but I could swear she was smiling. She started pulling up some hay and chewing it.

"She is *soooo* cute!" Mary Anne said.

"Can I pick her up?" Dawn asked.

"Me, too!" I chimed in.

We took turns holding her. Mrs. Stone was right. Elvira took to us pretty well. When we put her down, she'd scamper around and butt us on the legs. We would chase her, and she'd run away, dodging left and right.

"Oh, it'll be so much fun to take care of her," Mary Anne said.

"I know, she's a doll," Mrs. Stone replied with a smile. "Well, let me know what your parents say. I know this is an imposition — "

"I'm sure they won't mind," Dawn said.

"We'll ask them tonight," Mary Anne added. "And we'll call you."

"Fine," Mrs. Stone said. "Now I've got to give her her bottle."

"Bottle?" Mary Anne said. "Oooh, that is so adorable."

We said our good-byes and headed home. We couldn't stop talking about Elvira. Dawn and Mary Anne seemed pretty certain they'd get permission to goat-sit.

"I just don't know how we'll be able to wait till Saturday!" Mary Anne said.

Dawn sighed. "Imagine how we'll feel in three weeks. How will we be able to return her?"

"You could *kid*-nap her," I suggested.

"Very funny," Dawn said.

We gabbed on and on — what Elvira would eat, how we'd show her to our charges, what Tigger would think.

I wasn't the one who was taking care of Elvira, but I knew one thing — I'd be spending a lot of time at Dawn and Mary Anne's house in the near future.

A new teacher. A baby goat. The end of the school year. All in all, it was shaping up to be a pretty interesting few weeks.

CHAPTER 4

When I walked into math class the next day, Tom Cruise was in the room.

I don't know how he got there. I don't know what he was doing. I don't know how long he was going to stay.

But here's what I did know: My knees were weak. There was not enough air in the room. And I was not dreaming.

There I was, Stacey McGill, native New Yorker. I was used to celebrities on the streets of NYC. I could pass them by with just a casual glance.

But this was different. As I walked to my seat, I could not feel my feet touch the ground.

My brain? Total mush. I'd start to put a thought together, then HE would smile at something. Dimples would crease his cheeks, and I'd be gone. Lost. His slate blue eyes would flash across the room, and it was nuclear meltdown time. Then he'd run his hand through his wavy, light-brown hair, and I was afraid they would have to scrape me off the floor.

Do I sound like I was in *love*? I was. But somewhere, deep in the back of my pea-soupy brain, some little germs of reality were coming together. That guy could not really be Tom Cruise. Tom Cruise would not be standing in a math class at Stoneybrook Middle School. He would not be fiddling with a piece of chalk, talking to Mr. Z., glancing down at a sheet on the desk.

That didn't matter, though. It didn't change the way he looked, or the effect he was having on me. And I didn't figure out who he *really* was until Mr. Z. turned to the class and spoke.

"Okay, everybody," he said, just after the bell rang. "I'm pleased to introduce your new teacher, Mr. Ellenburg."

My heart stopped.

Tom Cruise was Wesley Ellenburg.

I had to let that idea sink in. I felt like an idiot for not having realized it right away. But I had an excuse. I had taken temporary leave of my senses. I could accept no responsibility for logic.

The name suddenly became cool. Much more interesting than, say, Tom Cruise. "Wesley" had a strong, intelligent sound. It reminded me of Wesleyan, where my dad went to college. "Ellenburg" made me think of a grand old Victorian-era village full of cobblestone roads, with a romantic park filled with hidden gazebos by a pond.

Puh-leeze! I said to myself. *Pull yourself together.*

And I did. Slowly. But I started to backslide when he spoke. His voice was as beautiful as his face. Not too high, not too low. Kind of breezy and confident, modest but strong.

"Uh, thanks, Mr. Zizmore," was what he said first. (I had never heard the name *Zizmore* sound so dreamy.) Then, as Mr. Z. took a seat in the back, Wesley Ellenburg continued. "Well, I'm happy to be here. This is something I've always wanted to do. Teaching, I mean — not sweating nervously."

He smiled bashfully at his own joke. The dimples! There they were. I let out a loud giggle. So did a few of the other girls. None of the guys seemed to think the comment was particularly funny.

"I'm a senior at SC," Wesley Ellenburg said next. "To get my B.A., I need to fulfill three weeks of student teaching. My favorite subject is math, so . . . well, here I am. I prefer a fairly informal class — lots of questions and discussions. And I plan to make myself available during study hall. . . ."

He went on and on. My mind digested

everything he said. A senior — that meant he was about twenty-two. Nine years older than me. Well, nine years isn't so much. When I turned eighteen, he'd be about twenty-seven. Two years after that, we'd *both* be in our twenties. And math was his favorite subject, so we had something in common.

". . . I once had a teacher who said, 'I have three names,' and he wrote *Mr. José Aviles* on the blackboard," Wesley Ellenburg went on. "He then said, 'Unlike most teachers, I let my students call me by my first name. So you can call me *Mr. Aviles.*' "

More laughter from the girls.

"Well, you can call *me* by my middle name," he said with that killer smile. "Wes. It's much simpler."

He wrote *Wes* on the blackboard. Peter Hayes made a big show of writing it diligently in his notebook. A couple of the boys snickered, but *Wes* just ignored them.

Wes.

Wild Wes.

How the Wes Was Won.

Calm down, Stacey.

Eventually we began math. He went over stuff I already knew, but I took notes anyway. It sounds goony, I know, but I didn't want him to think I wasn't interested.

And I truly was interested. He could have

been reading the phone book, and I would have found it *scintillating*.

This is what I learned during that class. Wes was right-handed. His left foot turned out a little more than his right. His sports jacket was tight around the shoulders. He tapped the side of his chin when he was thinking. And he was about the politest, most sensitive listener I had ever seen. He really did seem to enjoy answering questions, no matter how stupid.

But the big test came after Mr. Z. left. That was when Irv tried his foreign-exchange-student trick. "Zees x," he said, "ees zees nomber or letter? In mah contry, we do not hov zees." (Or something like that.)

Wes just stared at him for a moment. Then he nodded with a small, lopsided smile. "South of France," he said. "And not too bad. Can you do German?"

Well, after that, all the guys were on his side, too. I decided he was a talented teacher. Talented, cute, witty, warm, smart. Sigh.

Class lasted about nine minutes that day. At least it *felt* that short. When Wes began to give us his homework assignment, I began to feel the pang of separation.

The assignment was five word problems. As he dictated them, I wrote them down in my clearest handwriting. I dotted each *i* with a heart.

After the bell rang, I snuck a looooooong look at Wes while he was erasing the blackboard. I wanted to freeze him in my mind. In perfect detail.

" 'Bye, see you tomorrow!" I said, making sure to sound friendly but not overeager.

" 'Bye, uh . . ." He looked down at the attendance sheet.

"Stacey," I said. I was about to say *McGill*, but that would have been too formal.

"Stacey," he repeated with a self-conscious smile.

I needed all my concentration to leave the room in a straight line, without collapsing.

I floated to my locker, then raced outside to my BSC friends. We had planned to walk home together that day, even Kristy. (She was sitting for Marilyn and Carolyn Arnold after school, and they live near me.)

I told them about Wes. I don't recall what I said, but I remember Mary Anne beaming at me.

"Oh, Stacey, he sounds gorgeous," she said.

A breeze brought the scent of lilacs, so I closed my eyes and breathed in. Wes's face smiled at me in my imagination. "Drop-dead incredibly hunkified gorgeous."

"Hunkified?" Kristy repeated. "There's no such word."

"There is now," Claudia said in my defense. "I understand it. It's very . . . describatory."

"Descriptive!" Mallory interjected.

Claudia shrugged. "Whatever."

"What about Sam?" Mary Anne asked.

"Well . . ." I gave Kristy a guilty look.

She smiled. "It's okay. You're human. And sometimes, frankly, I'm not sure Sam is. My lips are sealed."

"Did you get his phone number?" Dawn asked.

"*Dawwwn*," I said. "I couldn't do that. He's a *teacher*!"

"Sabrina Bouvier went out with Mr. Jordan once," Kristy said.

"What?" the rest of us shot back. I couldn't believe that. Sabrina was *mature*, but still . . .

Kristy shrugged. "Well, it was a rumor."

"Ew," Jessi said. "How could you go out with someone so *old*?"

"That's like going out with someone your father's age," Mallory said.

"Or grandfather's," Kristy added.

"Wes is twenty-two!" I exclaimed.

Jessi nodded. "That's pretty old."

"Maybe he'll wait for you," Kristy said.

"You can prop him up as you go down the aisle."

This conversation was becoming way too silly. Besides, I didn't care what they said. Nothing could spoil the way I was feeling.

When I reached my house, I didn't even mind that my mom was at work. My cottage cheese tasted especially fresh. And I couldn't wait to start my homework — math first, of course.

I carefully read each problem. I worked them out on a sheet of scrap paper, making sure to use full sentences. I even included a few jokes, because I didn't want to seem too nerdy.

After double-checking a zillion times, I was positive my work was one hundred percent perfect. I copied it over in my best handwriting, and I had to restrain myself from planting a kiss on the first page.

(Well, there *are* limits!)

Then I thought of something *extremely* important. My clothes. I had gone to class wearing an oldish pair of stretch pants and an oversized turquoise men's shirt. Not awful, but not spectacular. There was no way I'd make the same mistake the next day.

I rifled through my closet. One by one, I looked at my best outfits.

Long red gown? Too dressy. Stone-washed

jeans (with a knit top)? Too casual. Paisley-print stirrup pants? Too faded.

I started the process at 4:35. By 5:05, I found myself staring at a short, rayon challis tank dress my mom had ordered for me. It was navy with white polka dots. The fitted top tapered down to a flared skirt, with white buttons down the front. It was feminine, yet comfortable-looking. Absolutely perfect.

I was dying to tell Claudia. I realized if I left right away, I could have a few minutes alone with her before the BSC meeting started.

I scooted outside, ran to the Kishis' house, and let myself in through the front door. (They leave it open on meeting days.)

I dashed upstairs, past Janine's room (as usual, she was hunched over her computer), and knocked on Claudia's door.

"Come on in!" Claudia said.

She was hard at work on a sketch. "Is it already time for the meeting?" she asked.

"No. I just had to tell you what I'm going to wear tomorrow," I blurted out.

"Why? Where are you going?"

"You know, to Wes's class."

I described the outfit. When I told her I was thinking of wearing thong sandals, Claudia suggested instead the new white sneakers I'd just bought, made of eyelet canvas with lace shoelaces.

"Ooh, good idea," I said. "Now, what scent does this outfit go with? Should I wear Lauren, or is that too, like, twentysomething?"

"I think it's fine," Claudia said. "But, uh, don't forget, Stace. This is a *class*. Wes is a *teacher*."

"I know, I know," I replied. "But Claudia, you should see this guy. I mean, in three weeks school will be over. What if he doesn't have a girlfriend? Who's he going to go to the beach with this summer?"

Claudia laughed. "Stacey, he's a *lot* older than you. He's graduating from *college*."

"I know," I said again. The room fell silent. Claudia gave me this understanding look. Then I had to ask her a question that was just burning in my mind.

"Do you know of a cologne with the scent of lilacs?"

CHAPTER 5

"Charlotte! Stacey's here!" Dr. Johanssen called upstairs. "And I'm leaving!"

"Okay!" I could hear Char's voice reply.

It was seven o'clock, at the end of a very long day. After the BSC meeting, I had run home for a super-quick dinner with my mom. Then I'd had to take my insulin and rush to my sitting job. (The life of a baby-sitter is never easy.)

Thump-thump-thump-thump-thump-thump. As Charlotte raced down the stairs, Dr. Johanssen gave me some last-minute instructions. Dr. Johanssen is Charlotte's mom, and she was on her way to the hospital. (Char's dad is an engineer, and he was working late.)

"Hi, Stacey!" Charlotte said. Her chestnut-brown hair bounced as she skipped into the living room.

"Hi, Char!" I said to my favorite charge.

Charlotte kissed her mom, and we all said

good-bye. As Dr. Johanssen pulled out of the driveway, I noticed something odd — a dark patch under Char's left eye.

"Uh, Charlotte?" I said. "Did you hurt yourself?"

Charlotte looked at me blankly. "What?"

"Your cheek looks bruised."

"Oh." She touched her left cheek and smiled. "It's just, um, a Magic Marker smear." Then she quickly added, "Can you help me with my homework? It's really hard."

"Sure."

We went upstairs. I noticed Char's books were closed on her desk. Next to them was a daisy with half its petals missing.

Charlotte opened a book and said, "We're having a spelling test tomorrow. Can you quiz me?"

"Okay."

She handed me the book and sat in her chair.

"How do you spell . . ." (I looked for a hard one) ". . . *porpoise*?"

When I glanced up, Charlotte was shoving the daisy into a looseleaf notebook. "What?"

"*Porpoise.*"

Char thought for a moment, then spelled it perfectly. That didn't surprise me. She is one of the smartest eight-year-olds I've ever met.

Plus she's funny and friendly and thoughtful and talkative.

She wasn't always like that, though. When I first came to Stoneybook, Charlotte was shy and glum. I guess I took a liking to her because she was an only child, like me. What caused her change? Her parents let her skip a grade (she was bored out of her mind by school). And, according to Char's mom, *I* was another reason she came out of her shell. I'm not sure that's true, but I sure felt good when I heard her say that!

"How about . . . *independent*?" I said.

No answer.

I looked up from the book. Charlotte was staring into space, her brow creased. "Char?"

"Um . . . independent," Charlotte repeated. "I-N-D-E-P-E-N-D-A-N-T."

"Almost," I said. "It's *E*-N-T."

We worked for awhile longer, but one thing was clear. Charlotte was not herself. She's usually quick with her homework and super enthusiastic. But she was neither that evening. She could barely focus on her spelling.

I was about to ask her what was up, when the phone rang. I ran downstairs and picked it up in the kitchen. "Johanssen residence."

"Hello, Johanssen residence, it's me," Claudia's voice answered.

"Claud, hi! What's up?"

Claudia sighed. "I just did my math homework with Janine the Genius."

"Uh-huh. So?"

"Well, she went into this big thing about how you have to 'look at the problem the right way.' So I listened. Then I looked at all the problems the right way."

"Well . . . that's great. Isn't it?"

"Fabulous. The trouble is, I still can't get the answers."

I sat down, found a pencil, and helped Claudia with *her* homework. When I was done, I went back upstairs.

Charlotte was not in her room. I figured she was in the bathroom, but I could see that the door was open and the light was out.

Tssst. Tssst.

The noise came from her parents' room, down the hallway. I walked down the carpeted hallway and peeked inside.

There she was, sitting at her mom's dressing table. Blush, eyeliner, and powder were all lined up neatly in front of her. She was holding a crystal atomizer, filled with perfume.

"Char?" I said gently.

"Oh!" Charlotte turned to face me. She put down the atomizer, then picked up a crumpled tissue and started wiping her face.

I smiled. *That* was why her cheek had looked

so strange. She'd been experimenting with makeup.

I sat down on the foot of the Johanssens' bed. Charlotte looked *very* worried. "You're not going to tell on me, are you, Stacey?"

I shook my head. "Nah. I remember doing the same thing when I was younger."

"You do?"

"Yeah. It was around the time I first discovered boys."

"Discovered boys?" Charlotte's face started turning a deep red — and it was *not* a reaction to the makeup.

"Uh-huh," I said.

Charlotte clammed up, but I had a feeling I knew what was going on. "Charlotte, I don't mean to be nosy, but may I ask why you're doing this?"

"I don't know," she said. "I guess . . . well . . ."

"Yeah?"

Charlotte took a deep breath. Looking down at the floor, she mumbled, "I . . . guzzala booskminzalil."

"What? Charlotte, I can't understand a word you're saying."

"I *said*, I guess I like Bruce Cominsky . . . a little." She rushed to add, "But I don't *love* him."

"Ohhhhh." I couldn't help smiling. First me

and Wes, and now Charlotte and some boy! Spring was definitely in the air. "That's *great*, Char! You have a crush — there's nothing wrong with that! Tell me about him. Is he cute?"

Charlotte giggled in a way I'd never heard before. Then she nodded a bit guiltily and said, "Yeah! He really is. He has red hair."

"Mm. That's nice," I said.

"And blue eyes," Charlotte quickly added. "And he says he hates girls, but I know he doesn't. His friend George told me he doesn't. And today he came all the way up to me on the playground. He *said* he just wanted to know if I saw his brownie, because someone took it. But I *think* he really likes me. Stacey, how can you tell if a boy likes you?"

I wanted to laugh. Boys are so strange, at any age. When Sam was first interested in me, he showed it by *insulting* me. "Um . . . well, sometimes it isn't easy. But sometimes you can just feel it. From the way he looks at you, or the things he says. Or if he goes out of his way to be near you — "

"He stuck out his tongue at me last week. But this week he did smile at me. Except he might have been laughing at me, because I stepped on some gum." Charlotte was talking a mile a minute now. I recognized the symptoms of acute crushitis. (I was very well acquainted with them myself.) "I don't know. Do you think I should say something to him? I mean, more than, like, 'Hi'? Every time I say that he kind of rolls his eyes."

"Well, boys can be funny — "

"I think another girl named Diane Dumschat has a crush on him, but he always says, 'Ew, Dumschat' every time she comes near him. So I know he doesn't like her." Suddenly Charlotte looked me straight in the eye. "Have you ever had a crush, Stacey?"

"Yes," I said. Now it was my turn to blush. "As a matter of fact, I have one right now."

Char's eyes lit up. "Really? Who?"

"A student teacher in my math class. His name is Wes."

"A *teacher*? Wow. Do you love him?"

"Well, *no*. I mean, it's too early to tell, Charlotte. Love is different than a crush. Deeper."

"Yeah? How can you tell if you're in crush or in love?"

I groped for an answer. "A crush is . . . something that hits you right away. Love takes longer. It has to grow."

"How long does it take? Does it *feel* like a crush? How do you know when it comes?"

"You just . . . *know*, I guess." I exhaled. "Uh . . . Char? Don't you have homework to do?"

A look of panic shot across Charlotte's face. "Uh-oh!"

She carefully put away the makeup and went into her room. I was off the hook. At the rate we were going, we'd have been up all night.

I helped Charlotte finish her work and get ready for bed. (We had a little more love/crush talk, and I found out about that daisy she had hidden. She'd been playing "He loves me, he loves me not" with it.)

After I said good night, I went downstairs to finish *my* homework. But Char's questions were sticking in my mind. How *could* you tell the difference between a crush and love? And what was this feeling I had inside? I assumed it was a crush, but it was so strong. All I could think about was Wes, Wes, Wes:

Wes and me in a rowboat on a romantic lake, floating to a mossy bank, where we set up a picnic and sit in the shade of a weeping willow.

Wes and me skiing on a crisp winter evening, schussing to the bottom of a mountain. We hang up our skis and then go inside for a candlelight dinner in a chic restaurant. Our faces are windburned, and we can't stop smiling and laughing . . .

By the time the Johanssens finally came back, Wes and I had traveled to Greece and Egypt, seen a Broadway show, kissed in the shadow of the Eiffel Tower, and had a brush with death on an African safari.

Getting paid and going home was an anticlimax.

But there was always Thursday. My homework was ready, my outfit was laid out.

I could not wait.

CHAPTER 6

I had three Hallway Sightings on Thursday.

One was on my way to homeroom. Wes was walking into the administration office, sipping coffee from a paper cup. Two was in the hallway between third and fourth period. Three was right after lunch, when I saw him through the open door of the teachers' lounge.

Yes, I spent the day on Wes Alert. And each time I saw him, he looked just as wonderful as he had the day before. He was wearing a navy blazer and khaki slacks. I love that look — and I was convinced that because we were both wearing navy, it had to be a sign.

I could also tell he liked my outfit. He didn't actually *say* he did, I just had an instinct.

But here's the best part. During class, he kept picking on me to explain math problems. The first time was a hard problem, and he seemed impressed when I got it right. Later he called on me to correct a wrong answer Erica Blumberg had given.

The third time was also to correct a wrong answer. When he said, "That's exactly right," he put on that smile, and I thought I would faint.

At the end of Thursday's class, he said good-bye to me — *by name*! I spent the rest of the day in a fog.

All in all, Thursday was a day of progress. I could sense a little electricity in the air.

I was sure sparks would start to fly on Friday.

From my secret psychological study of Wes, I had reached an important conclusion. He preferred dresses to slacks. So on Friday I wore a light, springlike sundress. As I walked into math class, Wes was shuffling through a stack of papers.

After the bell rang, he announced, "Today I want to talk about the homework assignment."

I froze. He didn't look happy. Obviously the class hadn't done well. Maybe the problems were all trick questions. Maybe I'd really blown it.

My stomach fluttered like crazy. Wes handed the assignments back in alphabetical order, so I was in the middle of the pile. The wait was excruciating.

When he came to my desk, I barely noticed the expression on his face. He placed the paper upside down, and I left it there for about a minute.

Finally, slowly, I picked it up and read the grade.

It said two things, in bright red ink:

A.

And *Perfect!*

I felt so relieved. My fluttery stomach was gone. I was smiling so hard my face hurt.

Then, after all the papers were handed out, Wes turned toward me. I grinned. He grinned back. He began walking to my desk.

This was it. I knew it. There, in front of the whole class, he was going to ask me out.

I put the idea from my head. It was *ridiculous*. But still . . .

He reached toward me, then gently picked up my homework assignment. Holding it up, he said, "These were not easy problems. I didn't expect anyone to get them all correct. But Stacey McGill had the one perfect paper in the class."

"Yea, Stace!" cheered Kara Mauricio.

"Big whoop," I could hear Irv mutter. (That's "whoop" as in "whoopee.")

The truth was, I felt kind of embarrassed to be singled out. But the moment I looked up I completely forgot my embarrassment. Wes was beaming at me!

A whole new world opened up that day.

Okay, I'm exaggerating. But my homework assignment paid off. I had become Wes's star pupil. Every time a really hard problem came up, he would pick me to work it out. I must have gone to the blackboard a dozen times.

The period whizzed by. When the bell rang, I felt depressed. I didn't know how I would make it through two whole days without math class.

On my way out, I passed Wes's desk. " 'Bye," I said. "Have a nice weekend."

He laughed and looked downward with a helpless expression. "If I'm not here the whole time."

I followed his glance. His desk was a disaster area. There were mimeographed notices, attendance sheets, homework assignments, open textbooks, and handwritten lecture notes on looseleaf paper. You'd think he had never heard of a paper clip.

"Whoa," I said. "It looks like a tornado came."

Ugggh. How could I have said that? I had made fun of his mess. *Just* what he wanted to hear. I felt like shrinking into the cracks between the linoleum tiles.

"Yeah," he said with a laugh. "You know, being a teacher is a lot different than being a student. In my dorm, I never put papers and books away if I'm working. Stuff piles up much faster here."

"You just need a system, that's all," I suggested.

He nodded. "Too bad I don't have a file cabinet."

"Can't you use Mr. Z.'s?" I asked. "Maybe there's room in it."

Wes looked behind him at the old olive-green metal cabinet Mr. Z. used. "I hadn't thought of that. I mean, it's *his*."

I shrugged. "Yeah, but you're the teacher now."

"Hmm. You're right." He pulled open the drawers, one by one. The bottom one was almost empty, except for about a dozen hanging file folders. "Heyyy, you are a genius!"

Genius?

The love of my life. The most beautiful girl I ever saw. The answer to my prayers. *Those* were some of the things I wanted him to say.

But genius was good. It was a start. I had to take what I could get.

Then Wes asked, "Um . . . do you have any plans right after school?"

Well, I almost died. The floor seemed to be moving and I felt as if I were about to keel over, out for the count.

But I stayed on my feet and thought fast. I was supposed to walk home with Mary Anne and Dawn, help prepare dinner, then go to our Friday BSC meeting.

60

"Nope," I said. "No plans."

"Good," he replied with the dimpliest smile in the world. My mind raced. What movies were playing? Did I have enough cash if we did dinner double-dutch? Were there still a few breath mints in my purse?

"Would you mind staying after a few minutes to help me sort these papers?" he asked.

And . . .

And . . .?

There was no *and*. That was it. He was waiting for an answer, and I was staring and gawking like a dork. "Oh . . . uh, sure," I said. "No problem."

Get a grip, I told myself. One step at a time. Let it build. First paper-sorting, then maybe a walk home, then a date for lunch at the mall.

Then Acapulco.

We worked for about forty-five minutes. I found Mr. Z.'s supplies, and Wes and I made a filing system. We figured out categories for all his junk, and organized it into file folders with color-coded tabs.

You know what? All talk of love and crushes aside, I really *liked* him. He made me feel comfortable. He was so gentle and relaxed. When we finished, he thanked me, we said good-bye, and I left.

By that time, of course, Dawn and Mary Anne had gone home. Which was just as well.

I probably couldn't have put together a coherent sentence if I had tried. I walked home alone, feeling ten miles off the ground.

At the BSC meeting later that day the first thing I did was explain what had happened and apologize to Dawn and Mary Anne for standing them up.

"Oh, that's okay," Mary Anne said. "We figured something like that had happened."

"Who's going to be the maid of honor?" Kristy asked with a sly grin.

"Can we bring Elvira to the ceremony?" Dawn said.

I could feel myself blushing. "Come on, nothing happened — "

"Yet," Claudia added.

"What *were* you doing all that time, hmmm?" asked Dawn.

"Just filing papers, that's all," I said.

"That's good," Kristy said. "Because you would not have believed the looks on the faces of the other girls in your class."

"What do you mean?" I asked.

"They came out while we were waiting for you," Kristy replied. "Erica was saying, 'I don't know why she has to hog him!' and stuff like that."

"Really?" I replied. "But I wasn't *hogging* him. *He* asked *me* to stay after."

Mary Anne suddenly spoke up. "Oh! Guess

what? I finally saw him today. Wes, I mean."

"What did you think?" I asked.

Mary Anne raised her eyebrows. "Well, I guess you were right when you said he is hunkified."

"But?" I said. "It sounds like there's a *but* coming."

"Well . . ." Mary Anne shrugged. "I mean, you know, I guess I prefer younger guys. That's all."

"Yeah," Jessi agreed. "You know what I figured? When you get out of college, Stacey, he'll be in his thirties." She said *thirties* as if she were talking about a geriatric.

Rrrrrrinnggg!

"Baby-sitters Club!" Claudia said in a businesslike voice.

We were off and running. During the rest of the meeting, the phone rang constantly. We didn't get a chance to talk more about Wes. As far as I was concerned, that was just fine. I didn't need to hear how old he was, or how many enemies I was making in class.

Frankly, I didn't care if Wes had a walker and a hearing aid. He and I had a relationship. It was starting slowly, but it was there.

Me? I was on Cloud Nine. Without a parachute.

CHAPTER 7

"O_w!"

Mary Anne pulled her thumb away from the barn's doorjamb. The nail she'd been holding clinked to the ground.

"Careful," Dawn said.

I picked the nail up and handed it back to Mary Anne, who was standing on the top rung of a ladder. "You sure you don't want me to do that?"

"Let me try one more time." Mary Anne held the nail against the wood again and drew back her hammer.

It was Saturday morning, the long-awaited day of Elvira's arrival. (Actually, we'd only met her four days before, so *short-awaited* would be more like it.) Dawn's mom and Mary Anne's dad were off running errands, so we had the whole place to ourselves. Dawn and Mary Anne had made a long banner that said WELCOME ELVIRA, and I was helping them drape it across the barn door. Inside the barn we'd hung some balloons, laid out some brand new tennis balls, and arranged a few baby bottles, wrapped in white ribbon.

I couldn't wait to see Elvira. Goat-sitting was going to be a new experience. Who knew what it could lead to? Especially if Kristy got involved. She'd probably want to tack up flyers on all the barns in the area. I could just see it: THE BABY-SITTERS CLUB — EXPERT CHILD CARE . . . and now, GOAT CARE!

Sort of gives "Kid-Kit" a new meaning.

I was enjoying the excitement about Elvira. It was keeping my mind off Wes.

(Well, not totally, but at least the weekend separation was less traumatic.)

Whack! Whack! Whack! "Ta-da! I did it!"

Mary Anne smiled at her expert nailing job. The banner was now in place.

She climbed down and we folded up the ladder. As we were storing it in the back of the barn, we heard the tooting of a car horn.

We ran out so fast, we almost broke our necks stepping on the tennis balls. Mrs. Stone had arrived in her pickup truck. Peeking out the passenger window was a tiny, bearded face.

"Hi!" we called out.

"We're here!" Mrs. Stone replied.

As she parked near the barn, we crowded

around Elvira. "Ooooh, she got even cuter!" Mary Anne said. "Can I take her out?"

Mrs. Stone slid out of the pickup and walked around toward us. "Go ahead," she replied.

Mary Anne opened the door and scooped up Elvira.

"Say hello, Elvira," Mrs. Stone said.

"Beeeeahhhh!" Elvira bleated.

"She's smart, too," Dawn said.

Mrs. Stone laughed. "My baby," she said, patting Elvira's head.

I looked into the pickup's rear section. All kinds of stuff was there — boxes, bales of hay, a long rope. "Can I help you with anything?" I asked.

"Yes, thank you." Mrs. Stone walked to the back of the truck and pulled open the pickup's gate. "Now, I've brought along her pen, where she'll sleep at night. I have more than enough food for her, so all you have to provide is her water. I also brought a collar and tether. Since your yard is not fenced in, you must make sure Elvira remains tethered to your barn."

"The whole time?" Dawn asked.

Mrs. Stone nodded. "As long as she's in your yard. Don't forget, a baby goat isn't a domestic animal. She could dart out into the road, get into your neighbors' garbage, even run away and get lost. But don't worry. I've brought a leash, too, in case you want to take her for a walk. And the tether is very long, so she'll be able to frisk around your yard. She won't even notice it."

"All right," Mary Anne said. I could tell she didn't like the idea of keeping Elvira tied up. (Neither did I.)

As we helped unload Elvira's stuff, Mrs. Stone went on and on with instructions: how often to feed Elvira, what to do if she spit up, how to care for her fur, how to change the hay in her pen. It was pretty complicated. (Elvira was adorable, but I admit I was glad Dawn and Mary Anne were the goat-sitters.)

Soon the pen was in the barn, the food was set up, and Elvira was tethered. Mrs. Stone finished her lecture and sighed. "Well, I guess that's it, baby," she said, picking up Elvira and kissing her on the head. "Ohhh, I sure will miss her. You know, I've been with her every day of her life."

Elvira gazed up at her. "Beeeeaaah?" Her voice sounded timid, as if she were asking a question, like "Why are you leaving me?"

"Yes, I know," Mrs. Stone said, cradling Elvira like a child. "But I'll be back soon."

Mrs. Stone's face started to turn red. Her eyes became watery. "Goodness," she said, "I — I didn't realize how hard this would be!"

Watching her, we were all a little choked

up. Mary Anne, of course, was crying. "Don't worry, Mary Anne," Dawn said. "You can stay."

That broke the somber mood. We all laughed, and Mrs. Stone finally put Elvira down.

After a flurry of further instructions she got back in the pickup and started backing down the driveway. "Good-bye!" she called. "You have my number in case you need me!"

"Okay! 'Bye!" we yelled back.

As the car disappeared down the road, Dawn and Mary Anne became the BSC's first official goat-sitters.

At first Elvira wandered around, looking a little unsure and scared. Dawn ran into the barn and brought out some tennis balls. She showed them to Elvira and said, "Want to play?"

Elvira cocked her head. "Beeeahhh!"

Dawn threw a ball toward the house. Elvira scampered after it. She planted her feet, kind of danced around the ball, grabbed it in her mouth and shook her head. Then she started rolling in the grass.

"She is so *cute!*" Mary Anne squealed.

Well, we must have used those words a thousand times that day. And not just the three of us, either. Pretty soon it seemed the whole neighborhood had found out about Elvira.

First the Prezziosos drove by. Jenny, who's four, started screaming, "Stop! Stop, Mommy! Look!"

The car came to a sudden halt. "Is it okay if she watches?" Mrs. P. called out.

"Sure!" Mary Anne answered. But it didn't matter what she'd said, because Jenny was already climbing out of the car.

Soon Buddy and Suzi Barrett came by, then Matt and Haley Braddock. At first we thought Elvira might get nervous with all those kids — I mean, *children* — around. But boy, did she prove us wrong. She loved them. She chased them, butting her head into their ankles. Then she'd run away in crazy zigzag patterns, until the kids fell on top of one another while Elvira bleated triumphantly. After that they played hide-and-seek, the kids screaming with joy every time Elvira found them.

At feeding time, Buddy held her in his arms and gave her a bottle, singing, "Hush, little Elvira, don't say a word, Buddy's gonna buy you a mockingbird . . ."

Mary Anne almost started to blubber at that sight.

Eventually Mrs. Barrett came to get her children — and they had a fit! She had to pull

Suzi away, kicking and screaming.

When they finally left, things became much quieter. Matt and Haley were trying to "trap" Elvira, signing instructions to each other with super-quick hand movements (Matt is deaf, so he and his sister communicate using sign language).

Dawn, Mary Anne, and I just watched, oohing and aahing and laughing.

At one point Mary Anne sighed. "I don't want Monday to come."

"Why?" Dawn asked.

"Between school and sitting jobs, we won't be able to see Elvira. I don't want to leave her!"

Haley let out a shriek of delight then — and I had a great idea. "Elvira would be perfect to *take* on jobs! We'd never have to worry about how to entertain our charges."

Mary Anne grinned. "That's right! And Mrs. Stone said we could take her away from the house if we put her on the leash!"

"I know," I said. "You could hitch her to a wagon and give goat rides!"

"Great idea," Dawn replied. "But we don't *have* a wagon."

"Oh," I said.

"Besides," Mary Anne added, "I think she's a little small for that."

We tossed around a few ideas, and that was

pretty much the way the rest of the day went. Chatting, playing with Elvira, enjoying the spring breezes.

As for Wes, well, I had a *small* daydream about him, a Heidi-and-Peter sort of fantasy, in which we were goatherds in the Alps together. But that was it. Really, I was happy as could be. I had my friends and some great entertainment. And I knew that as the weekend came closer and closer to an end, I could only feel happier. Because Monday would be nearer. And Monday was the first day of my first full week with you-know-who.

CHAPTER 8

Monday

Yesterday I sat for Jamie
Newton. Or I should say, I
was one of the hosts for the
Sunday afternoon Elvira
festival. I couldn't wait to
show Elvira off. I knew
Jamie would love her. I even
expected that other children
would show up.

I thought I was prepared.
I mean, I had Elvira's leash,
and I knew the children
would keep her occupied.
What could go wrong?

I just wish I had listened
to Mrs. Stone a little more
closely. Or taken a course in
Goat Psychology.

The Newton parents were going to visit Mr. Newton's brother. They were going to take Lucy, their baby daughter, with them, but Jamie had said he did not want to go. Dawn figured it would be a perfect job to bring Elvira on. Jamie Newton is four, and Elvira had already been field-tested with four-year-olds (Suzi Barrett and Jenny Prezzioso).

Not only that, but Claudia and Jessi both had jobs in the Newtons' neighborhood. Elvira could really be the center of attention.

Even so, Dawn made sure to be careful. Like a good BSCer, she thought: Never assume a parent will want a goat around the house.

So she called the Newtons. They didn't sound too thrilled about the idea, but Dawn assured them that Elvira was harmless and that Claud, Jessi, their charges would also come over. There would be plenty of supervision.

That did the trick. Dawn walked to the Newtons' house with Elvira behind her. Mrs. Newton greeted her at the doorway, wearing this doubtful expression. Lucy was asleep on her shoulder.

"Hi, Mrs. Newton!" Dawn said.

From inside the house, Jamie's scream drowned out Mrs. Newton's answer. *"They're heeeeeeere!"*

Now, Jamie is normally a mild, sweet four-year-old. But when he saw Elvira, he went *berserk*. He ran to her, laughing and shouting. Then he put his face up to hers and started bleating at the top of his lungs.

Poor Elvira backed away, looking scared and bewildered.

"Baaaah!" Jamie shouted. "Baaaaah!"

"Jamie," Mrs. Newton called from the front stoop, "take it easy!"

Jamie turned around to face her. Suddenly Elvira found her courage and lunged forward. She butted Jamie in the behind, shouting, "Beeeeahhh!"

Jamie stumbled. Mrs. Newton bolted out of the house. Lucy started crying. Dawn was mortified.

"Are you all right?" Mrs. Newton asked.

Jamie didn't say anything for a moment. Then a smile came across his face. "You know what Elvira did, Mommy?" he said. "She *butted* me in the *butt*!"

Jamie thought that was the most hilarious joke ever made. He doubled over with laughter. Mrs. Newton gave an uncertain smile. She looked carefully at Elvira and said, "I guess she's really too little to do any harm, isn't she?"

Dawn nodded. "And she loves children."

"Sssshhh, it's all right," Mrs. Newton whispered to Lucy as she took her back inside.

"Baaah! Baaah!" Jamie continued.

"Beeeeah!" Elvira answered.

Jamie jumped up and down. "See, we're talking!"

"Hi, Jamie!"

The voice from the sidewalk was unmistakable. The "hi" sounded like "hoi," which meant the Hobarts were coming over. (They're from Australia.) We looked up to see Mathew Hobart running toward us. His younger brother, Johnny, was close behind. (Mathew's six and Johnny's four.)

Behind them was Claudia. "Ooooh, she is so cute!" she gushed.

"Isn't she?" I gushed back.

It was a gushfest all around. The kids were having the times of their lives. Elvira ran around, butting and licking and generally being adorable.

Mr. and Mrs. Newton came out of the house. As they strapped Lucy into the car seat, they laughed at the scene in the yard. "Dawn," Mrs. Newton called out, "there's plenty of iced tea in the fridge. Help yourself! 'Bye!"

"Okay! 'Bye!" Holding tightly to Elvira's leash, Dawn waved.

As the Newtons backed out of the driveway, Dawn had some more visitors. Jessi came biking over with *her* charges — her eight-year-old sister, Becca, and Charlotte Johanssen. (Char and Becca are best friends.)

In unison they shouted, "Ooooh, she is so — " (Can you guess what the next word was?)

When Mal arrived with three of her siblings, Nicky (who's eight), Margo (seven), and Claire (five), it was unanimous. The verdict was "cute" on all counts.

Four sitters, eight charges, and a goat. It seemed like a pretty good balance. Elvira loved the attention.

"Can't you just let her run around?" Margo Pike asked.

"I wish," Dawn said. "But she's supposed to be on a leash at all times."

"Can I hold the leash?" Nicky asked.

"Ooh, me too!" Margo said.

"Me, too!" the others shouted.

"Whoa, wait a minute!" Dawn cried. "You can take turns — as long as you promise never to let go, and to keep her in the yard."

"Yeeeeeaaaah!!!!"

The kids all grabbed at once.

"Um, let's go in alphabetical order, okay?" Dawn said. "Becca, you're first."

As it dawned on Nicky that he was last, he stormed off, muttering, "That's not *fair*!"

He got over it pretty quickly, though. The

Newtons have a big yard, and the kids ran from one end to the other with Elvira.

When it was Johnny's turn, Mathew grabbed a plastic tablecloth from the Newtons' picnic table. He held it up and yelled, *"Toro! Toro!"*

I guess horned animals must share the same instincts, because Elvira charged like a bull. Laughing hysterically, Mathew pulled the tablecloth away. Of course, all the children wanted to try it. But when Claire tried, she couldn't pull the tablecloth away in time. Elvira went storming into it, pulling Claire along with her. Kid and kid went tumbling in a sea of red-white-plaid plastic.

Soon the others jumped in. As they rolled around, shrieking and laughing, Elvira calmly walked out. She stood there with that little goat-smile and bleated.

We cracked up. It looked as if she were making fun of the kids.

After awhile Claire pulled a jump rope out of her pocket. "Can Elvira skip rope?" she asked Dawn.

Nicky slapped his head. "Not while she has a leash on, bubble-brain!"

"I'm not a bubble-brain, you silly-billy-goo-goo!" Claire retorted.

They went off to settle their argument, Elvira scampering after them.

"Who wants iced tea?" Dawn asked.

She was answered by a chorus of "me's."

"I'll help," Claudia volunteered.

Together they went into the house. They found a huge pitcher of iced tea in the fridge and put it on a tray with a stack of paper cups.

They returned to a yard full of happy, *loud* children. Jessi and Mal were in a deep conversation, but they stood up to help pour the drinks.

Becca was the first to come up to the table. " 'Scuse me," she said, pulling on Dawn's shirt.

"Here you go," Dawn said, handing a cup to her.

"Thanks," Becca replied. "But, uh . . . where's Elvira?"

"Nicky has her," Dawn replied. She looked around the yard. Margo and Charlotte were trying to get a kite in the air. The Hobart boys were throwing a Frisbee with Jamie Newton. Nicky was tormenting Claire, holding her jump rope high in the air and making her reach for it.

"Gimme!" Claire screamed.

"Nicky?" Dawn said. "Where's Elvira?"

Nicky kept dangling the rope and pulling it away. "I don't know," he said.

"You don't know?" Dawn repeated. "Nicky, you had her last!"

Nicky stopped his game and looked toward the house. "She was — um, I thought she was playing — "

"You let go of the leash?" Mal asked.

Nicky nodded guiltily.

"Nicky!" Mal scolded.

Claire took the opportunity to grab the jump rope. "You tweetie-bird brain!" she yelled.

"All right come on, let's form a search party," Jessi said.

"Yeah! Search party!" Mathew replied.

"Let's split up," Dawn said. "Jessi, you take Becca and Char toward Brenner Field and look everywhere. Mal, you and Margo and Nicky and Claire look around the yard and the garage. Claudia, you and the Hobarts look across the street. I'll take Jamie and look around the neighborhood."

Operation Elvira began. The neighborhood echoed with Elvira's name and lots of "baaah"-ing.

Dawn and Jamie went from house to house, looking in front and backyards. When they reached Bradford Court, they passed Claud's house.

"Elvira!" they shouted.

CRAASSSHHH!

They stopped short. The sound came from the Goldmans' house, next door to Claudia's.

Dawn and Jamie ran toward the house. The

Goldmans' garage door was open, and their car was gone. But the floor was strewn with rotting banana peels and coffee grinds and paper trash. "Oh, bad, *bad* goat!" Dawn yelled.

She ran inside. Elvira was there, all right, standing by a large, overturned garbage can. She was happily chewing on a salad of ripped newspaper and spoiled food scraps.

"Eeewww!" Jamie cried, and then dissolved into giggles.

Dawn grabbed Elvira's leash and pulled her away.

"Beeeeaahh!" Elvira protested.

It was a good thing Elvira was a baby. She dug in her heels, but Dawn was able to pull her to the Newtons' yard. "I found her!" she yelled out.

When everyone had returned, Dawn went back to the Goldmans'. She rang their bell but no one answered, so she went into the garage, found a broom, and swept up the mess. She carefully dumped everything in the garbage can. Then she closed it tightly and made sure there were no signs that anything had happened. She was petrified the Goldmans would find out. They're an older couple with no children, and last year their house was broken into and robbed. Dawn didn't want them to think the same thing had happened.

The rest of the day passed by without any

tragedies. But later on, as Dawn was walking back to the Newtons' with Elvira and Jamie, she noticed the Goldmans' car was in their driveway.

She began to feel guilty. She remembered how upset Mrs. Goldman had been about the burglary. What if she noticed something "off" about the garage? Would she and her husband search around, thinking something had happened? Would they call the police?

Dawn pulled Elvira across the street. "Come on, Jamie," she said.

"Where are we going?"

With a sigh, she replied, "To the Goldmans'. We're going to confess our crime."

"Huh?"

Jamie looked as if he were about to cry when Dawn spilled the beans to the Goldmans. But as it turned out, they laughed at the story and invited Dawn and Jamie in for a fruit snack.

And Elvira feasted on fresh banana peels, right there in the comfort of the Goldmans' kitchen.

CHAPTER 9

On Wednesday, Wes and I celebrated our one week anniversary.

We didn't do anything special in class. No cake or party favors. It was a private celebration, in our minds only.

At least in *my* mind.

Wes was subtle. He waited till the end of class to pop the question.

Well, not *the* question, but *a* question.

"Stacey," he said in his honey-coated voice as I was walking out of the room, "would you mind lending me some of your organizational skills again for awhile?"

Erica was passing by me at the time, and you should have seen the look on her face. I thought her eyes would pop out. I could hear her mutter something to Maria Jonaitis on the way out the door.

I felt awkward. I wanted to run after her

and talk to her. We'd always been friendly, and I hate making enemies.

But then I looked at Wes. Somehow, instantly, Erica became a distant memory.

"Um, sure, I guess so," I said (as if there had been any doubt). Actually, I didn't have anything important to do before the BSC meeting.

"Great! Your filing system was so good, I ended up putting away everything the minute it landed on my desk. The problem is, I guess I was supposed to fill out some of those papers and return them."

"Uh-oh . . ."

Wes ran his fingers through his hair. "Yeah. Mr. Kingbridge stopped me today wanting to know where my W4 form was, and my insurance form, and my progress report — forms I didn't even know I had."

"Oh, no. What did you tell him?"

"I told him I'd get them to him before he left today." Wes exhaled and shook his head. "I shouldn't have let him intimidate me like that. Sometimes I'm such a wimp."

Ohhh. I wanted to squeeze him and tell him it was all right. He looked so vulnerable.

I hadn't seen this side of Wes until that day. I thought he was the type who never let anything bother him. Now I was catching a glimpse of the true Wes. Strong but sensitive. Confident but sometimes unsure.

Human.

I fell in love with him all over again.

"Don't worry," I said. "Just tell me what to do, and we'll finish in time."

"Okay, have a seat." Wes turned and pulled open the file cabinet. He flipped through his folders, taking out sheets and putting them on his desk. "Ah, here's something you can use your math skills with. I need to have everyone's grades averaged. Why don't you do that while I fill out my W4 . . ."

He gave me a list of grades. (First he folded the names over so I wouldn't know which grades were whose.) I felt excited. I was determined to figure out the averages without using a calculator.

Not to mention the fact that I could tell which grades were mine. And guess who had the highest average in the class? Ta-da!

There was plenty more to do after I finished the averages. Some of it was just filling out forms, but I found out a lot more about Wes that way — like his Social Security number, his birthdate (August 19), his mother's maiden name (Stratten), his official height (five feet eleven) and weight (one hundred sixty-one pounds), and his blood type (O positive).

As I was filling out the last form, Wes

checked my averages. "I knew it," he said with a smile. "Absolutely perfect!"

I looked up, trying not to smile like a goon. Out of the corner of my eye, I saw the clock.

Five-eleven.

"Oh, no!" I said.

"What?" Wes whipped around as if I'd seen a burglar.

"We've been working for over two hours! I have to go to a meeting." I explained the Baby-sitters Club to him and frantically gathered my things together.

"Uh . . . look, this was my fault," Wes said. "Why don't you let me drive you? We'll drop off my forms at Mr. Kingbridge's desk, then we can go straight to the parking lot."

"Okay!" The word leaped out of my mouth, halfway between a squeak and a shout.

This was a dream come true. I was going to ride to Claudia's house side by side with Wes Ellenburg.

In his car.

Alone.

I managed not to scream and make a fool out of myself. I was cool. I was composed.

I picked up Wes's class record book and headed for the door.

"Uh . . . you don't need to take that home," Wes said.

"Huh?" I looked down and felt horrified.

"Oh! Sorry, I — I thought — I was in such a hurry, I — "

Wes picked up my books and handed them to me. "That's okay. Let's fly."

He grabbed his stack of filled-out forms, and we ran into the hallway. On the way out, Wes dropped off the forms with Mr. Kingbridge's secretary.

Moments later, we were running toward The Car. It was a battered silver-gray Toyota Corolla with a Stoneybrook University sticker across the rear windshield. The bumper was held on by rope. "Meet Winston," he said as he opened the passenger door.

"Winston?"

He smiled shyly. "That's my car's name. It's seven years old, but it drives beautifully."

Then he held the door open for me and waited for me to get in. What a gentleman!

"Toyotas are my favorite cars," I said as I sat down. (They were, too. I had just made the decision.)

Wes gallantly shut the door behind me. "Well, you may change your mind after it starts moving."

He ran around to the driver's side and slid in.

We were sealed now. Together in our own world.

I gave Claud's address to Wes, and he

started the car. We pulled out of the lot and drove onto the Stoneybrook streets. What a feeling! Wes and I were in the real world now — away from school.

I was psyched. I wanted to shout. I wanted the whole town to see me. It was a good thing Wes didn't have a convertible, or I might have floated right out the top.

How was the ride? Bumpy, I think, but I couldn't tell. The bumps might have been the beating of my heart, which felt like a jackhammer.

Wes drove beautifully. He could do so much at once. While he talked, his legs worked the clutch and accelerator. He reminded me of a church organist making music with foot pedals. We chatted about school, he told me some jokes, then he turned on the radio.

And when he sang along with a love ballad, I thought I'd die. He had a gorgeous voice!

Then it happened. He touched me.

It was only a brush on the hand, but it sent a shiver right through me, until my toes tingled. His hand casually continued on to the stick shift, and he pulled it down.

Did he really need to shift right then? I didn't think so. My heart raced. The Touch was intentional, it had to be.

I turned toward him and gave him a smile. He was looking straight ahead. I wasn't sure if he saw me. All I could think was: is it possible? Did he feel for me the way I felt for him? Had he kept me after school so long on purpose, knowing he'd have to drive me somewhere later?

It wasn't a far-fetched idea.

Finally Wes did turn toward me. He looked me in the eye and smiled. My tongue felt like a wad of cotton. "Well . . ." he said with a shrug.

I practiced my reply in my head: *A date? Of course!*

" . . . here we are," he ended his sentence.

Oh.

I hadn't noticed the car had stopped. I looked out the window and saw Claud's house. "Thanks for the ride," I said, barely getting the words out.

"You're welcome," Wes replied. "See you tomorrow."

"Okay. 'Bye." I got out of the car and stabilized myself. As Wes drove off, I waved to him.

As I walked up the path to the front door, I didn't know if my heart would explode before my knees gave way.

I don't remember actually walking into Claudia's room, but I do remember Kristy asking, "What happened to *you*?"

"Hmmmm?" I replied.

"Don't scare us, Stace," Claud said. "Are you having a blood-sugar problem, or is this something . . . Wes-related?"

"He drove me here," was all I could answer as I sank onto the bed.

Mallory was wide-eyed. "He did?"

"Mm-hm . . ."

"*And?*" Mary Anne insisted.

"And I think he likes me."

"Really?" Dawn said. "What did he say?"

"It's not what he said," I replied. "He let his hand brush against mine. In the tenderest way."

"Wowww . . ." Jessi said.

I leaned back against the wall. The clock clicked to five-thirty and Kristy forgot to say "Order." She — and the other members of the BSC — were staring at me.

I guess they had finally realized nine years wasn't such a big difference, where true love was concerned.

CHAPTER 10

~~There are~~ I see two stars in ~~the summer's~~
night, ~~Far away floating.~~ blinding
Hovering, lost, ~~even in all the night the~~
light
Each ~~is~~ so dull in ~~the sky~~ heaven's
~~web pool network~~ net.
~~Thus~~ So each remains, ~~not in over~~
~~the school because~~ as yet
~~they never not~~ unmet
But ~~luck~~ Fortune ~~happens~~ moves in
strangest ways, ~~And now it~~
It lengthens nights, it shortens days,
May this night end, and ~~this~~ day begin
And bring two lovers back again.

N_o.

No *way*!

I crossed out *lovers*. Who was I kidding? If Wes read that, I would be *mortified*. Even if he did like me.

I wrote *people*. Then I added the word *young* before it. The last line read *And bring two young people back again*.

It wasn't quite right. The rhythm was off.

Arrrrrrgh.

It was nine-thirty. I had been writing the poem since right after dinner. This had to be the twentieth draft.

It started out as a good idea. I needed some way to let out all the feelings that had been building up. I was too embarrassed to admit them to Mom. There was only one person I wanted to tell, and that was Wes.

But I couldn't do that. At least not directly.

That was when I'd thought of writing a poem. At first I wrote about him and me, but that was too obvious. Then I changed the names, but somehow it sounded silly.

Then I remembered a phrase we read in *Romeo and Juliet* in English class: "star-cross'd lovers." That gave me the idea of comparing Wes and me to two stars.

I tried to make my poem sound like Shakespeare. I figured Wes was the kind of guy who read Shakespeare. But I couldn't decide whether I liked the poem or not. It was hard to *see* it through all the cross-outs.

Maybe there's a good reason why math was my strong point.

I began looking in my desk for some nice paper to copy the poem onto.

"Stacey!" my mom called from downstairs. "Phone!"

"Who is it?" I answered.

"I don't know," she said. "Some boy."

I shot out of my seat and ran to the door. "A boy?" I said, keeping my voice low. "You mean, like a *boy*, or a male, you know, who might not be a boy?"

My mom chuckled. "I don't know, Stacey. It sounds like someone your age, but I can't be sure."

"Okay," I said. "I'll take it up here!"

I ran into my mom's room. Could HE be calling? Oh, my heart. I took hold of myself. I sat by the phone. I forced myself to stop shaking.

Then I picked up the receiver and clamped my hand over it. "I have it!" I shouted. "You can hang up now!"

I quickly put the receiver to my ear and waited for the click. Then I swallowed and said, "Hello?"

"Hi, Stacey," said a male voice. "It's Sam."

"Sam?" I squeaked.

"Yeah, Sam." He laughed. "You know, as in Thomas."

"Oh." I felt like a flat tire. "Hi, Sam."

"Um, I was calling because, well, Kristy was telling me about the Spring Dance at your school."

"The Spring Dance?" I hadn't even thought of it. I'd forgotten it existed. Between Elvira and Wes, there had been so much going on.

"Yeah. I was wondering if you needed a date for it. If you do I could take you."

My mood picked right up. What a sweet-heart. Things had really cooled off between us, and I thought he'd forgotten about me. And I still did *like* him. I was about to say "Sure!" In fact, my mouth was forming the "sh" sound when I stopped.

I couldn't say yes. What if I did, and then Wes asked me? True, we weren't going out. But I was sure he had feelings for me, and after he read this poem . . .

"Oh, Sam," I said gently. "You're sweet to ask. But I'm already going with somebody."

I hated, *hated* to lie. And I felt so guilty. But what else could I do?

Sam's voice grew very soft. "Okay. Just thought I'd try. See you later."

"Okay. 'Bye."

" 'Bye."

I hung up and sank back on the bed.

If this didn't work, I was going to feel like such a jerk.

But it was going to work. I was determined to show Wes the poem. Once he read it, he'd know exactly how I felt. If he really was holding *his* feelings for me inside, he'd be able to tell me.

I marched back into my room. I rooted around in my desk and pulled out some special stationery that I've hardly ever used. It's white parchment paper edged with lace. Then I found my pen that writes in gold ink. At the top of the page I wrote *For Wes*.

In my best handwriting, I made a clean copy of the poem.

I see two stars in summer's night,
Hovering, lost, in blinding light,
Each so dull in heaven's net,
So each remains, as yet unmet.

But Fortune moves in strangest ways;
It lengthens nights, it shortens days.
May this night end, and day begin
And bring two young people back again.

There. The poem was finished. And I had to admit, it was pretty good. I couldn't believe *I* had written it.

Sigh. Isn't it amazing what love brings out?

I placed the poem carefully in a manila envelope, closed it, and sealed it (with a kiss).

Then I started my homework. It was almost bedtime, but I *had* to do at least my math. In the week since Wes came, I hadn't gotten even one problem wrong on any assignment. I wanted to maintain my record.

I carried the poem with me all day Thursday. In fact, I had put the manila envelope inside a bigger manila envelope. That way, when it came time to give the poem to Wes, I could hand him a clean envelope without any smudges or wrinkles.

I wanted to run into him during the day. Then I could give him the poem, forget about it for awhile, and hope that he'd read it before math class.

But good old Fortune was not kind to me that day. I didn't see Wes at all until class.

When I walked in, we said hi as always. As always, he handed back an assignment and we discussed it. As always, the class was fun and interesting.

Only Wes and I knew about what had happened the previous evening. He managed to keep cool about it, and so did I.

The class flew by. By the time the final bell rang, I was beginning to have second thoughts. What if Wes didn't like the poem? What if he didn't *get* it? Did it need another verse? Were there too many words in the last line?

I knew that if I hesitated I'd never give it to him. So I reached into my shoulder bag and pulled the envelope out of the envelope. As the other students were leaving the room, I walked straight to Wes's desk.

Wes smiled at me. "Stacey, thank you so much for helping me yesterday. You kept me out of trouble with Mr. Kingbridge. I hope you weren't late for your meeting."

"Nope," I said. "And you're welcome. Um, by the way, I wondered if you would, uh, look at this."

Wes gave me a curious frown and took the envelope. Then, as I stood there petrified out of my mind, he opened it and began to read the poem.

I watched him carefully. I was not breathing. My heart had decided to check out for a few moments. Wes's frown deepened, then disappeared.

For the life of me, I couldn't read the expression on his face. He was staring at the poem, just staring.

Then, quickly, he put it back in the envelope. "Thanks, Stacey," he said with a strange kind of half smile. "It's . . . uh, beautiful. Um, jeez, I'm going to be late for a staff meeting. Sorry to run. See you tomorrow."

With that he rushed out the door.

And he took my poor frozen heart with him.

CHAPTER 11

Tuesday

I brought Elvira to the Barretts' house today. I'd remembered how much Buddy liked her the day she came to stay at my house.

Today also happens to be Day 10 of Elvira's visit.

Well, after 10 days, Dawn and I still love Elvira — even though she hasn't been exactly predictable. We've also figured out how to deal with her on sitting jobs. But you know what? Elvira wasn't the only impossible one today.

Well, in writing that, Mary Anne was very kind to Elvira. You want to know the truth? That cute little goat had turned into a pain in the neck.

She was still sweet-natured and frisky and goofy. But she had this incredible appetite for garbage.

The incident at the Goldmans' was only the first. Part of the problem was the size of her pen. Dawn and Mary Anne didn't have the heart to keep her cooped up in there all the time. They preferred to leave her in the yard on the tether. Unfortunately, it was hard to keep the garbage cans out of her reach.

Practical Mr. Spier tried to solve the problem by buying a new set of cans with clasp handles. That didn't work. Elvira figured out how to open them.

Needless to say, Elvira had some pretty interesting dinners on the sly. Some of them were *so* interesting that she decided she needed to see them again after she ate them. (That's all I'll say without getting too gross. You can figure out what I mean.)

One other problem. With so many little tidbits of food lying around, the barn became a favorite hangout for other forms of wildlife. Field mice, raccoons, squirrels, bats, yellow jackets — Elvira had many callers that week.

She found the Braddocks' garbage during one sitting job, but she didn't do too much damage. Fortunately the parents were just as good-natured about it as the Goldmans had been.

Let's face it, it was impossible *not* to like Elvira. She didn't make trouble on purpose. She wasn't bad-tempered. She was just . . . being a goat!

Anyway, on Tuesday (yes, almost a week after I gave Wes the poem, and no, he hadn't said a word about it) Mary Anne called Mrs. Barrett and asked permission to bring Elvira on her sitting job. Mrs. Barrett agreed — but she forgot to tell her kids about the arrangement.

So when Mary Anne showed up, they went absolutely wild. Well, two of the three did.

"Aaaaaah!" Buddy screamed when he saw Mary Anne through the screen door. "Look who Mary Anne brought!"

He barged outside, bleating at the top of his lungs.

"Who?" Suzi said, wandering to the door. Then, another happy "Aaaaaaah!" and *she* came running out, bleating even louder.

Next came Mrs. Barrett and Marnie. Now, Marnie is only two, and she wasn't around the day her siblings met Elvira. Plus, she wasn't expecting this weird-looking animal to show up at her house.

Elvira was a bit too much for her. Marnie took one frightened look out the door and started crying.

Oh, great, Mary Anne thought. She figured she'd have to take Elvira home, which would mean Mrs. Barrett would have to wait for her. She would be mad about *that*, and Buddy and Suzi would be mad that Elvira had to leave. And if there's one thing Mary Anne likes to avoid, it's conflict.

Fortunately, before Mary Anne could burst into tears, Marnie calmed down. Mrs. Barrett led her slowly out the door by the hand, saying, "That's a goat, Marnie, can you say *goat*?"

"Doat," Marnie said.

"Beeeeaahhh!" Elvira replied.

Marnie froze. Then she looked up at her mother. "Beeeeahhh!" she repeated.

It was a *great* imitation! Buddy and Suzi exploded into giggles. Marnie looked quite pleased with herself. She let go of her mom's hand and walked right up to Elvira, saying "Beeeeahhh!" again.

This time Elvira scampered away. Then she looked back at Marnie as if to say "Follow me!"

Marnie understood. She started chasing Elvira, laughing hysterically and calling "Doat!"

101

Mary Anne knew then that everything was going to be all right.

It was, too, for about the first hour after Mrs. Barrett left. Then Buddy came up with a brilliant idea. "Hey, Mary Anne," he said. "Did you ever teach Elvira to pull a wagon?"

"No," Mary Anne replied.

"Well, let's try. We have a wagon!"

"Oh, I don't know, Buddy," Mary Anne started to protest. "She's so small, and — "

"Yeah! Yeah!" Suzi yelled. "It's a small wagon. It's a teeny tiny wagon. Really. I'll get it!"

Before Mary Anne could reply, Suzi had disappeared into the garage. She came out pulling a small, red-slatted toddler-type wagon.

"Wagga! Wagga!" Marnie cried.

"See? See how small it is?" Suzi said.

"All right, all right," Mary Anne replied. "Come on, Elvira."

She took Elvira's leash and pulled her toward the wagon. But Marnie had chosen that moment to play "chase-me" with Elvira. Unfortunately for Mary Anne, Elvira had decided she was in love with Marnie — and she had grown stronger over the ten days of her high-protein garbage diet.

Each time Mary Anne would start to hitch

the leash to the wagon, *whoops!* Off went Elvira, and off went Mary Anne with her.

Finally she managed to tie the knot. Elvira moved forward, and the wagon rolled along.

The Barrett kids laughed and clapped their hands. "I know!" Buddy said. "We can charge kids a quarter for a ride with Elvira!"

"Yeah!" Suzi cried. "Let's go get Claire and Margo and — "

"Just a minute," Mary Anne said. "Let's see if Elvira can do it first. She's just a baby, you know."

"She can do it!" Buddy insisted. "Come, Elvira! Come to Buddy!"

Well, at first Elvira didn't take to that wagon at all. Each time she felt its tug, she'd stop and look confused. Then she'd try to shake it off. Then she'd turn and butt it.

After awhile, though, she seemed to get used to the idea. Marnie was chosen to be the maiden passenger on the goat-cart.

But with the added weight, Elvira could not move it an inch. "Beeeahhh!" she complained.

"Sorry, Buddy," Mary Anne said. "I'm afraid it's not going to work."

But Buddy was deep in thought. "I know! We can charge kids a quarter for their *picture* with Elvira."

He ran into the house and emerged minutes

later with a Polaroid camera. "See? We can use this!"

"Buddy," Mary Anne said patiently, "the film in that camera costs a lot more than a quarter per picture."

"That's okay," Buddy replied. "I'm allowed to take pictures with it whenever I want. Right, Suzi?"

"Right," Suzi said.

"White," Marnie agreed.

The cards were stacked against her. Mary Anne had to say yes.

Buddy led them through the neighborhood, like the Pied Piper (the Pied Photographer?). Lots of neighborhood kids were willing to pay a quarter for a photo. Buddy ended up making two whole dollars.

And Mary Anne ended up worrying that Mrs. Barrett would be mad about the film.

Oh. Guess who was one of Buddy's customers? Charlotte Johanssen. And she was full of news for Mary Anne. She had finally decided to declare her love to Bruce Cominsky. She had written him . . . a poem!

And can you guess what his reaction was? He fell hopelessly, madly, in love with Charlotte. He started writing her poems. At least three a day. He called her at night to recite them to her. In fact, he wouldn't leave her alone. Now Charlotte wasn't so sure *she* liked *him* anymore.

Now, you know how I feel about Char. I dearly love her. I always will. But I couldn't help thinking that some girls have all the luck.

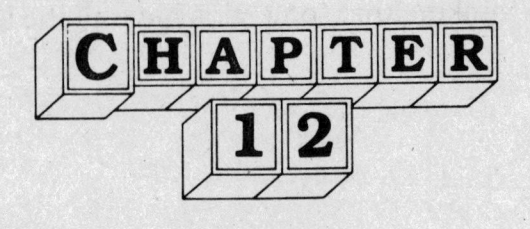

CHAPTER 12

I was going out of my mind.

It was Thursday. I had given Wes the poem a whole week ago. I sat in math class, trying to work out the problems he had written on the board, but I could not concentrate.

Had I missed something? Had he tried to give me a sign? If not, then why hadn't he said anything? Did he hate my poem? Had he forgotten about it?

I needed to know how he felt. Even if he felt nothing. The *not knowing* was eating me up inside.

The paper on my desk was a blur. I blinked once, twice. It became clear.

Over and over, on the lines, in the margins, around the holes, I had written *Wes*. And I hadn't even been aware of it.

This had gone way too far. Wes was going to be teaching for another entire week. At this rate, I'd be a vegetable by then.

I decided I had to tell him. Face to face. No matter how *he* felt, I had to make *my* feelings known. It was the only way I could feel like a person again. A poem could be taken many ways. A poem was vague. I had to be direct.

When the bell rang at the end of class, I stayed in my seat. I waited for everyone to leave. Soon Wes and I were alone. He was busily erasing the blackboard.

"Oh! Stacey!" he said as he turned around. "I — I didn't know you were still here. Sorry."

He was *so cute*. I tried to speak, but my lips wouldn't move.

"Do you have a question about the assignment?" he asked.

I managed to shake my head.

He shrugged and began to look uncomfortable. "Do you . . . um, have another poem?"

"No," I said. My voice was thin, and I had to swallow. Thoughts were tumbling around in my brain. At least he remembered the poem. But what did he mean by that question? Did he really *want* another poem? Was he *hoping* to get one? Was he making fun of me? I was so confused.

"No, I don't have another poem," I said. "I usually don't write poems. I sort of . . . put everything I had into that one."

Wes was just staring at me. That same blank stare he'd had when he read the poem.

"You know," I went on, "I meant every word of that poem. It was about you and me. It was about my feelings. In case you haven't noticed, I have a crush on you." I took a deep, deep breath. "No, that's not it. I — I think I'm in love with you, Wes."

There it was. I had said it. Finally it was off my chest. I felt light-headed. I felt relieved.

I felt sick to my stomach.

Wes turned about three shades of pale. His eyebrows shot up. He looked at the floor.

It was the worst thing I could have expected. He was shocked. *He hadn't known.* Obviously he didn't feel the same way about me. All this time, I was just a smart math student to him. Nothing else.

Nothing.

I couldn't stay in the room. I didn't want him to see me cry.

I picked up my books and ran out the door.

Thank goodnesss for Claudia. I called her when I got home that day, blubbering like a baby. She came over and comforted me. She made me some tea and told me jokes. I am lucky to have such a great best friend.

I vowed to myself that the next day, Friday, I would wear pants to school for the first time in two weeks. Who cared if Mr. Wesley Ellenburg liked dresses? Besides, how did I know how he felt about clothes, anyway? I had completely misjudged his feelings about *me*, hadn't I?

By the next morning, I had begun to have second thoughts. Maybe I hadn't misjudged Wes's feelings. Sure, he was a twenty-two-year-old man, but that was still young. Everyone knows boys mature more slowly than girls. Maybe he was confused. Maybe he found it too hard to talk about feelings. Maybe he liked me so much he couldn't find the words to say so.

I wore the polka-dotted tank dress to school that day.

I didn't see him until math period. To tell you the truth, walking into class did make me feel happy. I was embarrassed about my emotional display, but I really did feel a huge burden had been lifted. And poor Wes seemed much more uncomfortable than I felt. He could hardly look me in the eye.

At the end of class, minutes before the bell rang, he made an announcement. "Well," he began, "this has been my last full week with you. I truly have enjoyed it."

There was some applause in the room. I joined in.

Wes grinned shyly. "Thanks. Just so you know, I'll teach through Wednesday, then Mr. Zizmore will take over till the end of school, which is the following Tuesday. But I'll probably see some of you on Friday night, because I've agreed to be a chaperone at the Spring Dance."

The Spring Dance! I'd forgotten about it.

What a bummer. I had no date. Wes was out of the question, and I'd blown it with Sam. Amanda Martin, a girl in my class, had asked him — and he'd accepted!

I slumped home after class. Later on, at the BSC meeting, I hardly said a word. I could tell Claudia had told the other club members what had happened. Everyone was very, very gentle with me.

I had a chance to think a lot about Wes that weekend. Here's what I thought: After Wednesday, I might never see him again. I might never know if he liked me. After all, *I* had walked out on *him* Thursday. He hadn't said anything. I needed to give him a chance to open up. Who knew? I might be surprised.

At any rate, I didn't have anything to lose.

On Monday morning I spotted him entering the building. "Hi, Wes!" I called out.

"Oh, hi, Stacey," he replied.

He was smiling. He wasn't avoiding me.

"Ready for your last three days?" I asked. A dumb question, I know, but I couldn't think of anything else to say.

"Yeah," he answered. "But I'm really going to miss you — you know, your class."

I'm really going to miss you. He said it. He may have meant the class, but something made him say those words.

"Well, see you in class," I said.

"Okay, see you."

Hold on, Stacey McGill, I thought. There's hope.

Sure enough, Wes seemed much more relaxed in class that day. I made sure to ask him for help from time to time, and he was cool about it. He even smiled at me twice.

Tuesday was even better. When I ran into him after lunch (okay, I admit I looked for him), he was smiling from ear to ear.

"You look happy," I said.

"I am," he replied. "Can you keep a secret?"

"Sure!"

He leaned close and lowered his voice. "I found out from Mr. Zizmore that I'm getting the highest recommendation possible!"

"Yea! Oh, that's fantastic! You really deserve it."

"Well, it helps to have great students in the class, like you."

"No, you're just good, Wes. Congratulations!"

"Thanks. See you in class!"

" 'Bye!"

Wes had confided in me. Told me a deep secret.

Hope. Hope. Hope.

Finally Wednesday came. Do-or-Die Day. I didn't know what to expect. I wasn't sure what I would say to Wes.

I saw him in the hallway that morning. "Wes!" I called out. "Hi. How do you feel?"

"A little nostalgic, a little happy," he replied.

"I — I wonder if I'll see you . . . after this," I said. "You know . . . around?"

Ugh. Very weak, Stacey.

"Uh, well, maybe!" Wes replied, suddenly looking as if he were late for something. "Anyway, I'll see you at the dance on Friday!"

As he jogged away, I just stood there and beamed.

Yes. Yes. It might happen.

It just might.

CHAPTER 13

Friday

   I sat for my brothers and sisters yesterday. Dawn sat with me. Everyone was happy to see Elvira. She really is cute. She may not have a future on the stage, but she is cute. However, I have a new problem on my hands. Now Vanessa doesn't want to be a poet any more. After yesterday, my sister is convinced she'd rather be a playwright...

Remember when I said that Mallory Pike has seven brothers and sisters? A few of them had been at the Newtons' on the day Elvira was temporarily lost. But there are plenty more. I'll mention them in order:

You know Mal. Then there are the ten-year-old triplets (Adam, Jordan, and Byron), Vanessa (who's nine), Nicky (eight), Margo (seven), and Claire (five).

As you can imagine, sitting for them is a big job. Which is why Dawn was sitting with Mal that Thursday, the day before the Spring Dance.

Dawn had not *planned* to bring Elvira with her to the Pikes'. Looking after all those kids would be work enough. But Mary Anne was sitting at the Prezziosos', and there was no question of bringing Elvira there (Mr. and Mrs. P are very fussy). The poor little goat had spent the day all cooped up, and Dawn felt sorry for her.

Besides, the Stones were due to come home the next day. Elvira would have to go back to the farm. Dawn didn't want to spend any more time away from her than necessary.

And that was how Elvira ended up at the Pikes'.

As usual, the kids went wild. As usual, Elvira was in top form, butting and playing and running around.

Everyone had an idea for Elvira. "Let's dress her up!" Margo said.

"Let's hitch her to a wagon!" Nicky suggested. (He's friends with Buddy Barrett.)

"Let's bring her to a movie!" Claire exclaimed.

But it was Vanessa who came up with the idea of the day. "I know!" she said. "I'll write a special version of *The Three Billy Goats Gruff,* and Elvira will be the star. Then we can put the play on this afternoon for all the kids in the neighborhood."

This was met with instant approval.

"Wait a second," said Mal the Writer. "Are you sure you can write this by the time Dawn has to leave?"

Vanessa nodded. "Sure!"

"And set up a stage, and rehearse?" Mallory added.

"No problem," Vanessa assured her.

"We can help," Byron said.

"I'll tell the neighbors," Adam added.

"Me too," said Jordan.

"Nicky and I can make a stage," Margo volunteered.

"Okay, okay," Mal said. "Let's set a time. Dawn has to leave at five o'clock. Vanessa, when do you think the play will be ready?"

"Um . . . four-thirty?"

"Okay. Adam, you'll remember to say that to everyone?"

"Yup!" Adam, Byron, and Jordan sprinted off to spread the word.

Vanessa disappeared into the house to write.

Nicky and Margo began dragging lawn chairs out of the garage.

And Claire was happy to have Elvira all to herself.

Dawn and Mal sat back and watched the preparations.

Margo and Nicky spent a long time figuring out what to use as a bridge. First Nicky brought out a sled from the garage, but Margo thought it was too low. Then Margo suggested a ladder, but Nicky pointed out that they'd never get Elvira to climb on it.

Finally they decided to use a small, wooden ladder-slide that Claire had played with as a toddler. At the top of the ladder was a platform with handles, and under the platform was a hiding place big enough for a troll.

At three-thirty Vanessa emerged from the house with a pencil behind her ear and a pad of legal paper in her hand. "Okay," she said. "I'm ready! Let's choose parts. We need a troll and two goats."

All three triplets wanted to be the troll. Margo, Nicky, and Claire each wanted to be goats.

"Whoa," Dawn said. "Can we double up some parts?"

Mal read the script. She came up with a perfect casting solution. Since the troll comes out three times, once for each billy goat, she suggested that Adam, Byron, and Jordan take turns playing the troll. Elvira could be the smallest billy goat, Nicky could play the bigger billy goat, then Margo and Claire could team up to play the biggest billy goat.

"Okay, get in place for rehearsal!" Vanessa snapped. She pulled a visor out of her back pocket and put it on, backward.

"I guess she's the director," Mal said to Dawn.

"I call being the first troll!" Jordan yelled.

"I call second!" Byron said.

"Hey, no fair!" Adam cried. "Let's go alphabetically."

"You *always* say that," Jordan complained.

Vanessa's first job was to organize the trolls. She decided on reverse alphabetical order, so Jordan did get his way. He ducked under the platform.

"Lights, camera, action!" Vanessa said. "Bring in Elvira!"

As Dawn pulled Elvira toward the slide, Vanessa held up the script. " 'Once upon a time,' " she read, " 'there were three billy goats who lived by a stone bridge, and their last name was Gruff. They ate all the grass on their side of the bridge, so they had to cross to the other side. But a gross, ugly, slimy troll lived under the bridge — ' "

"Hey!" Jordan said.

"It's only a *play*, stupid!" Vanessa shot back. Then she continued, " 'So one day the smallest billy goat, Elvira Gruff, started over the bridge, *trip-trap, trip-trap* — ' Okay, Dawn, that's where you bring in Elvira."

"All right." Dawn began pulling Elvira toward the slide.

Well, you'd think the slide was a ring of fire. Elvira would not go *near* it. Finally Dawn picked her up and gently placed her on the platform. *"Beeeeeeahhh!"* Elvira bleated.

"Ssshh, it's okay," Dawn said.

"Come on," Jordan called from below. "It's getting hot down here!"

Elvira seemed startled by the voice. She tried to scramble away. Dawn lifted her again and calmed her down. "Uh . . . I don't know if this is going to work," she said.

"She'll be fine," Vanessa insisted. "I have an idea. Let's make her the last billy goat. That way if she messes up, most of the play will be over."

"But she can't be the *biggest* billy goat, dumbhead!" Adam said. "She's the smallest of us all."

Vanessa turned and stuck out her chin. "Who's the director, you or me?"

Grumbling, Adam backed off. The Pikes ran through the play, with Vanessa yelling out the lines. The kids did pretty well — and Elvira was a *little* better. She still had to be lifted onto the platform, but that was all right. All Elvira *really* had to do was stand there. The neighborhood kids would be thrilled just to see her.

At four-thirty the audience began to arrive: Marilyn and Carolyn Arnold, Jenny and Andrea Prezzioso (with Mary Anne), Haley and Matt Braddock, and several of the Hobart boys. At the last minute Charlotte Johanssen came by.

"Hi, Char!" Mal said. "What are you doing in this neighborhood?"

Charlotte rolled her eyes. "Trying to hide."

"Hide?" Mal repeated.

"Yeah." Charlotte looked over her shoulder. "From this boy named Bruce. He came over to my house, but I told my dad and mom to tell him I was out."

"How come?"

"He's a pest! He keeps following me. You know what he did after my mom told him I was gone? He stood under my window and started yelling, 'Roses are red, red's the same as scarlet; Sugar's sweet, and so is Charlotte,' over and over at the top of his lungs!"

Mal laughed. "That's cute."

"It's embarrassing!" Charlotte insisted. "So that's why I snuck out the back door and ran away."

"Ladies and gentlemen and goat lovers of all ages!" Vanessa suddenly shouted. "Welcome to a Pike Production presentation of a Vanessa Pike play, *The Three Billy Goats Gruff*, starring Elvira Goat."

"Yeeeaaaa!" the crowd yelled.

Vanessa began her narration. Then Nicky came over the bridge, saying *"Trip-trap, trip-trap."*

Jordon the Troll jumped out and bellowed, "Who's trip-trapping over my bridge?"

"Me, the smallest billy goat," Nicky said. "I'm going to the other side to get fat."

"Then I shall eat you up — *nyah-ha-ha!*" (What a ham.)

"No, please don't. Wait for my sister goats instead. They are fatter than I am. Like, humongous and blubbery."

"Hey!" Margo shouted from the garage. "That line isn't in there!"

Scowling, she and Claire came out with a sheet draped over them. Up the bridge they

120

went, *trip-trap, trip-trap*, only to be stopped by Byron.

Eventually it was Elvira's turn. This time when Dawn pulled her, she scampered toward the slide. But instead of climbing the stairs, she put her head down and rammed into the cramped little space where Adam was hiding. "Hey! Stop!" Adam yelled.

"Elvira!" Dawn called.

But Elvira was determined to be with Adam. She crowded herself inside, trying to find some little area in which to hide.

Adam was whooping with laughter. "That tickles!"

He tried desperately to get out, but he couldn't. So he just stood up. The slide rose off the ground and toppled over. Adam and Elvira collapsed in a heap.

"No! No! No!" Vanessa yelled.

The audience *loved* it. Matt Braddock laughed so hard he fell off his seat.

Elvira got up and ran away, trailing her leash behind her. She disappeared behind the garage.

"Come back!" Dawn shouted.

"My play!" Vanessa moaned.

Then . . . *crash!*

"The garbage!" Mal and Dawn yelled.

They ran after Elvira and found her standing happily in a pile of rotten food.

Behind them they heard a chorus of "Eeeewww!" (The entire audience had followed the show to its new location.)

Mal said the disgusted look on Dawn's face was priceless. She and Mary Anne burst into laughter.

"Well," Mary Anne said as she pulled Elvira away. "I guess Elvira's never going to get an Oscar."

Dawn picked up the garbage can and sighed. "Yeah, unless it's an Oscar the Grouch."

All in all, I think my friends were just about ready for Mrs. Stone's return.

CHAPTER 14

"I'm home, Stacey!" my mom's voice echoed through the house.

I put away my makeup and ran downstairs. "Did you remember to bring it?"

Mom laughed. "You only called three times to remind me. Of course I did! I hung it on the shower rack."

"Thanks!" I said. I gave her a quick kiss and ran to the bathroom.

It was Friday, a half hour before the Spring Dance. Mom and I had gone shopping at Bellair's after school. With her employee discount, she had been able to buy me one of the most beautiful dresses I had ever seen. (I had had to run straight to the BSC meeting afterward, so she held onto it at work.)

I stood in the bathroom and admired it. It was a calf-length silk/cotton dress with pastel floral print, a scoop neck, and a shirred skirt that was slit to above the knee on one side.

"I *love* it!" I cried out.

"I know!" Mom replied.

I took it to my room and changed. Then I checked my makeup in the mirror, slipped on my bracelet and silver hoop earrings, and stepped into my flats. I pulled my hair back and fastened it with a ribbon.

I was ready.

"Watch out, Wes," I said to the stunning blonde in the mirror.

No, Wes had not asked me to the dance. I was going doe. (That means alone. Well, guys go stag, so why can't girls go doe?)

Claud's date was Austin Bently, Mary Anne's was Logan, and Mallory's was Ben Hobart. The rest of us — me, Jessi, Dawn, and Kristy — were dateless. (Bart Taylor, Kristy's sort of boyfriend, couldn't make it.)

But you know what? I didn't care.

Because I would be free. Free to dance with Wes. Free to talk to him, woman to man.

I had realized what our problem was. As a teacher, he was forbidden to get involved with students. There were probably rules about that. That would explain his silence — I was always trying to talk to him in *class*, where anyone could see us. He was worried about being kicked out.

But now the school year was ending. Maybe Wes would be able to open up. At the dance

I would draw him out, find out what was on his mind. Find out what was really behind those incredible make-me-melt smiles.

See you at the dance Friday night.

Those words kept repeating in my head. He had said them to me. I knew it was a harmless statement, but he didn't *have* to have said it. He could have said, "See you in class," which had been what he usually said. But no. He had specifically mentioned the dance to me.

He had something he wanted to tell me, I just knew it. And I was dying to find out what it was.

I flew downstairs.

"Oh, Stacey, you look gorgeous," Mom said.

"Thanks!"

I felt gorgeous. It was a gorgeous night. As we rode to the school, I rolled down the windows and let the air fill the car with the scent of spring.

The school was lit up and decorated with balloons and banners. Kids were hanging out on the front lawn, watching the sunset.

I said good-bye to my mom, walked across the lawn, and entered the gym. What a transformation from earlier in the day! Jonquils and tulips and daffodils were twined around the pillars, streamers had been draped from the basketball hoops, and a beautiful SMS SPRING

Dance banner hung from the ceiling, hand-painted in pastel colors.

A deejay was busily working in the corner, and the music was already blaring. Around the room, people had started to dance.

The first BSCer I ran into was Jessi. "Wow, what an outfit!" she said.

"You, too!" I replied. Jessi looked sensational, in an indigo blue unitard with a matching open-mesh oversized cardigan.

"I think I see Mary Anne," she said, "over by the punchbowl."

But my eyes were already there. A group of teachers and chaperones was standing a few feet from Mary Anne. In the middle of the group was Wes — wearing a tux.

Yes, a tux.

I don't know about you, but tuxes make me weak. I think men are born to wear them. Take the world's dullest guy, put him in one, and he'll look cool. Take Wes . . .

I could not stop staring at him. And Jessi knew it. "Oops," she said with a giggle. "The girl is *gone!*"

"Oh, sorry, Jessi," I said.

"It's okay, go ahead!" she replied. "I see Mal coming in, anyway."

I couldn't say no. I walked up to the punchbowl, picked up a glass, and tried to look as if I were just *so* thirsty for Hawaiian Punch mixed with ginger ale (which I couldn't even drink in the first place).

The adults were laughing about those adult things that never sound very funny. Wes would soon be bored with them, I was sure.

As the gym began to fill, the teacher/chaperone group split up. And Wes turned toward the punchbowl.

"Hi!" I said. "Want to dance?"

I had no fear. It was tonight or never.

And you know what? Wes didn't look away, or shuffle his feet, or talk about math.

He smiled and said, "Sure!"

We stepped onto the floor. A really hot rock tune was playing, and the beat was practically shaking the room. All around us, people were dancing like crazy — Mary Anne and Logan, Mr. Zizmore and Mrs. Rosenaur, Kristy and Mr. Fiske (which meant I wasn't the *only* BSCer dancing with a teacher). In the corner about ten girls were dancing with each other, laughing and singing to the music.

"What a great song!" Wes said.

"Yeah!"

We started to move to the music. Instantly I found one more thing to love about Wes. He was *such* a cute dancer. His moves were natural, but not super smooth. He had great rhythm, but no fancy footwork. And he looked as if he really *enjoyed* dancing.

When the song was over, he flashed his dimples and said, "You're terrific!"

"Thanks." I was glad the lights had been turned low. I hoped he couldn't see my face turning red. "You, too . . . for a teacher."

"For a teacher!" He threw his head back and let out a loud laugh. "We'll see about that! Let's dance this next one."

A breath caught in my throat. Now *he* was asking *me*! The next song was even faster. It was one of my favorite dance songs (even though I was sort of hoping for a slow dance).

Wes really cut loose. And so did I. We jumped and whirled around the gym. The lights and decorations swept by in a bright-colored haze. I could sense people staring at us. A lock of hair fell across Wes's forehead. I pulled out my ribbon and shook loose my hair. Wes was laughing. I was laughing.

Oh, I was in heaven. I had never felt this way with a guy. I could have died right there, and I would have been happy.

My heart was pounding when the song finished. Wes was flushed in the face. His chest was heaving from the effort. His hair had fanned across his forehead, making him look even cuter (if that was possible).

"Whoa!" he said.

Before I could reply, Kara Mauricio walked up to us and said, "You guys were amazing! Can I be next?"

Wes pulled out a handkerchief and wiped his brow. "Sure!" he said. "Thanks, Stacey."

"Thank *you*."

We shared a smile. I walked back to the punchbowl. I tried not to mind that Wes was dancing with Kara. I mean, she was his student, too. She had a right. It was just a dance.

I waited by the table, catching my breath. I was thirsty, and I found a sugarless alternative to the punch, but I didn't feel like drinking. I wanted to be ready when the dance was over. I wanted to be ready if Wes started looking for me.

But the dance floor kept filling up, and I kept losing sight of him.

The next number was a jitterbug. When I saw Wes, he was talking to Ms. Harris, a science teacher (unmarried, but *much* older than Wes). Unfortunately, they started dancing.

I walked closer. I was determined not to lose him for the next number.

Ms. Harris was a great jitterbugger, and I could tell Wes was having a good time. A couple of times he caught my eye. He knew I was there.

Then it happened. Just what I wanted. A slow song began, and someone dimmed the lights even further.

The floor started to clear. Only the serious couples stayed. I could see Mary Anne and Logan embracing.

Wes was heading in the opposite direction. I walked up behind him and tapped him on the shoulder. "Wes?" I said.

He turned around. "Oh, hi, Stace," he replied. He sounded out of breath, and his face was still sweaty from the jitterbug. "Ms. Harris was pretty amazing, huh? For a teacher!"

I smiled. He was using my joke. "Wes," I repeated, "will you dance with me?"

"Well, uh, whew, I'm kind of winded from that last one. I think I'll sit this one out. How about the next song?"

I looked him deeply in the eye. "The next one might not be so . . . slow."

Oh lord, what had gotten into me? The words had come out of my mouth, as if they'd had a life of their own.

Wes took a deep breath. "Stacey, I think we'd better have a talk."

I felt my stomach bounce like a water balloon. The blood rushed from my head. I opened my mouth and a very thin "okay" came out.

Wes walked to a dark corner of the gym. I

followed, putting one shaky leg in front of the other. I felt as if something were exploding inside me. Something that was a little like joy and a lot like fear.

When Wes turned around, he was smiling. But it wasn't the same smile he'd had on the dance floor. It wasn't even the same smile he'd had in math class. I couldn't read it at all.

"Uh, Stacey," he said. "I don't want you to think I've been ignoring what you said to me last week."

"Uh-huh," I managed to say.

"I did understand your poem. And it was beautiful. It — it just took me by surprise, that's all. I didn't know what to say."

"Well . . . do you know now?"

Wes nodded. "Yeah." He took another deep breath and ran his fingers through his hair. "Stacey, you are a brilliant, talented, attractive girl . . ."

Uh-oh. I didn't like the sound of this.

"But I think you have an idea about . . . you and me that's not the same idea I have."

"What idea?"

"Well, that we can have a relationship. We can't. I mean, it's not that I don't like you — "

"Then what is it, Wes?" I wanted so badly to cry. This was going all wrong.

Then something dawned on me. Something I should have suspected from the beginning.

"Oh . . . you have a girlfriend, right? No, wait. You're *married*, aren't you?"

"No," Wes said, shaking his head. "No steady girlfriend, no wife. It's just that, well . . . you're *thirteen*, Stace. That's far from a little kid, I know. But that's also far from twenty-two. Farther than you think. Too far."

"Mm-hm," I said. "I understand."

The look in Wes's eyes was so warm, I couldn't be angry at him. Even though he was breaking my heart.

"Good," he replied. "We can be friends, can't we?"

I forced my lips into a smile. It was like lifting a house. "Yeah. Sure, we can. Thanks for talking to me. I'm going to go get a drink now."

"Okay. 'Bye, Stacey. And thanks for the dances."

"Yeah. They were fun. 'Bye."

I did not shake as I walked away. I made sure to control myself. No way was I going to run off crying in front of all those people. I was going to stay and enjoy the dance.

At the punchbowl I poured myself a drink. It went down as if I were swallowing sandpaper. Through the blur of the tears I was trying to hold back, I saw Amanda Martin dancing with Sam. The guy who could have been my date. Who was handsome and nice and fun and fifteen years old — and who *used* to like me.

I saw Wes, too. He was with a bunch of the younger teachers. No students were around them. He looked so comfortable. How could I ever have thought . . . ?

That question lingered in my mind the rest of the night. I could push it aside from time to time, if I was with people. So I tried to be around my friends and dance as often as possible.

But whenever I found myself alone, the question was still there. And when the dance was over, it pounded in my brain like a rock song that wouldn't stop.

I left without even looking at Wes Ellenburg. I felt as if he'd reached right inside me and ripped me apart.

Outdoors, the cool air calmed me down. Mom was supposed to pick me up, but she hadn't arrived yet. I looked into a sky crowded with stars. I thought about my poem.

And then, in the dark of the moonless night, I felt the tears start to roll down my cheeks.

CHAPTER 15

I went to Dawn and Mary Anne's the next day. The Stones were coming home, and they wanted a big send-off for Elvira.

I have to say, Elvira was not the first thing on my mind Saturday morning. I was a mess. I had no urge to get out of bed. I think if Dawn hadn't called to invite me over, I might have stayed there all day.

As I walked up the street, I was still stinging from what had happened at the dance. I could not believe how I had deluded myself. I felt so stupid.

I hoped Elvira would take my mind off Wes.

Dawn and Mary Anne were in the yard. So were Mal and Kristy and a bunch of the neighborhood children. Everyone was crowded around something (Elvira, I assumed). They were all laughing hard. The WELCOME ELVIRA banner was back on the barn, only it had been changed to say WE'LL MISS YOU ELVIRA.

"Hi!" I called out.

As everyone turned to say hello, I heard a loud "Beeeeaaahh!" Elvira scooted out from beneath Kristy's legs and ran toward the barn.

She was wearing a frilly bonnet, and a half-tied red bow hung from her tail.

"Hey, come back here!" Dawn called out. "We're not finished."

"Beeeeaaahh!" Elvira was dipping her head and trying to pull off the bonnet with her hoof.

"Noooo! Don't!" Mary Anne cried.

Everyone raced after Elvira, trying to convince her to cooperate. But she wouldn't. Before long the bonnet lay on the ground, dirty and ripped.

"So much for that idea," Kristy said.

The neighborhood kids lost interest and went home.

I sat on the grass and watched Elvira for awhile. Mary Anne went into the house and returned with a bottle. "Feeding time!" she called out.

Elvira scampered over to her. Mary Anne scooped her up and sat down on the back stoop. As she began feeding Elvira, she started to cry.

"Are you okay?" I asked.

Sniff, sniff. "Yes," Mary Anne replied. "It's just that — " *Sniff, sniff.* "This is the last feeding I'll ever give her."

"Ohhhhh." I sat down next to Mary Anne. I put my arm around her shoulder. It felt nice to comfort somebody.

Soon Jessi joined us, then Claudia, and then Logan. Logan brought a box of Kleenex. ("I know when to come prepared!" he said.)

Claudia had a bag full of — what else? Junk food. Only it was all for the guest of honor.

Elvira loved the Doritos and Twinkies and Snickers, hated the Milk Duds, left half the Chunky bar, and went nuts over the wrappers that hold Reese's peanut butter cups.

Mr. Spier and Mrs. Schafer fixed us all a lunch of chicken salad sandwiches. We sat at their picnic table and gabbed away between bites. We were about halfway through when we heard a loud honking in the driveway. "Hellooo!"

The Stones' pickup truck had arrived. I could hear Mary Anne gulp.

Then the driver's door swung open and Mrs. Stone got out. She was grinning from ear to ear. "Where's my little baby?"

"Beeeeeaaahhh!" Elvira trotted out from behind the picnic table. She stopped when she saw Mrs. Stone. For a moment I thought she'd turn and run.

Instead, she bleated again and *sprinted* into Mrs. Stone's arms. Mr. Stone stepped out of the car and stood next to his wife. He was a heavy-set man with a receding hairline and a big smile. "Oh, she got so *big!*" he said.

"What kinds of yummy food have they been feeding you?" Mrs. Stone asked.

You don't want to know, I thought.

Mrs. Stone looked around at the gathering. "How sweet of you all to show up! And what a wonderful banner. I don't know how to thank you, Mary Anne and Dawn. Was she any trouble?"

Mary Anne valiantly attempted to answer the question. "N — " *Sniff, sniff.* "N — " *Sniff, sniff.* "N — "

"Not at all," Dawn said. "She charmed the whole neighborhood."

Mr. Stone chuckled. "I don't doubt it. She probably ate everybody's trash, too."

We howled at that.

Out of the corner of my eye, I saw Charlotte wander into the yard. I turned and gestured for her to come over.

"Well, thanks again," Mrs. Stone said. "And you are *all* invited to come to the farm any time to visit Elvira and the other animals."

As the Stones walked back to the car, we shouted good-bye. They loaded Elvira and her belongings into the back and drove away.

Mary Anne was a basket case. I noticed she'd already made a huge dent in Logan's tissue box.

I didn't blame her. As I watched the pickup putter down the street with Elvira's little pointy head sticking out the back, I felt pretty choked up, too.

Charlotte stuck her hand in mine. "Guess what, Stacey?" she said with a big grin.

"What?" I asked.

"Bruce Cominsky doesn't bother me anymore."

"Congratulations. What happened?"

"I guess I've been running from him so long he just gave up. Now he has a crush on Diane Dumschat."

"You mean, as in, 'Ew, Dumschat'?"

"Yeah!"

I laughed. "Go figure."

"What?" Charlotte said, wrinkling her brow.

"Boys are hard to figure out."

"No, they're not. They're just dumb. It's stupid to even think about them."

Good point. I wish I could have thought of that a few weeks ago.

Charlotte ran off to play, and I said my goodbyes. I had promised to help Mom around the house.

Claudia walked home with me. She could sense I was sad. We hadn't talked since the dance, so I filled her in on all the gory details.

When I finished, she shook her head and

said, "You know, you didn't do a thing wrong, Stacey."

"You don't think so?"

"Of course not. You couldn't help it. You can't stop your feelings from happening."

I looked at the ground. "I think I loved him, Claud. I really do."

Claudia fell silent for a moment. "Well, at least you did something about it. You told him how you felt. It would have been worse if you had kept it in."

"Ohhh, why does love have to be like that? Horrible if you keep it in, awful if you let it out."

"Not always, Stacey," Claudia said gently. "People do fall in love together. It happens to almost everyone sooner or later. It just didn't happen that way for you this time."

I sighed. "I guess sometimes love hurts."

"Yeah," Claudia said with a nod. "I guess so."

We walked the rest of the way home without saying another word.

About the Author

ANN M. MARTIN did *a lot* of baby-sitting when she was growing up in Princeton, New Jersey. Now her favorite baby-sitting charge is her cat, Mouse, who lives with her in her Manhattan apartment.

Ann Martin's Apple Paperbacks include *Yours Turly, Shirley; Ten Kids, No Pets; With You and Without You; Bummer Summer;* and all the other books in the Baby-sitters Club series.

She is a former editor of books for children, and was graduated from Smith College. She likes ice cream, the beach, and *I Love Lucy;* and she hates to cook.

Look for #66

MAID MARY ANNE

I finished my tea in a sort of whirl of energy and feeling good, jumped up and cleared off the tea cups and saucers, washed the pot, and put everything away. Then I went to the back door and picked up the water can just outside. "Why don't I water the plants on the porch?" I suggested.

"Oh, Mary Anne, thank you. They've been getting mighty thirsty and I just am not able to give them the attention they need."

I not only watered the plants, but I swept the porch and the kitchen. "The kitchen is probably ready to be mopped," I said tactfully (I hope). "You want me to just . . ."

"Oh, no, no, no, no. I couldn't . . ." Mrs. Towne's voice trailed off and she looked at me thoughtfully. Then she said, "Mary Anne. Instead of paying me for sewing lessons in money, why don't we do some good, old-fashioned bartering?"

She went on and said, "Like why don't I swap you sewing lessons for some help with these chores. I've got to face it. I just can't do them with my ankle like this."

"That's a great idea, Mrs. Towne. That is — if you think it is fair. I don't mind helping you a bit."

"I know you don't, but I'd feel much better if we did it this way. What do you think? Is it a deal?"

"It's a deal," I said.

"Great. Now, let's do a little more of the fun work — sewing — before the day is over."

"Why don't I put a load of laundry in while you get set up in the sewing room," I suggested. "Then I can put it in the dryer before I go."

"Perfect," said Mrs. Towne.

And that's the way I felt as I walked home after my sewing lesson. Perfect. It had been fun. I was learning new things. And I was going to be able to help Mrs. Towne out, too.

Perfect. Just perfect.

**Read all the latest books
in the Baby-sitters Club series
by Ann M. Martin**

146

by Ann M. Martin

More titles... ➧

☐ MG44970-2	#49 Claudia and the Genius of Elm Street	$3.25
☐ MG44969-9	#50 Dawn's Big Date	$3.25
☐ MG44968-0	#51 Stacey's Ex-Best Friend	$3.25
☐ MG44966-4	#52 Mary Anne + 2 Many Babies	$3.25
☐ MG44967-2	#53 Kristy for President	$3.25
☐ MG44965-6	#54 Mallory and the Dream Horse	$3.25
☐ MG44964-8	#55 Jessi's Gold Medal	$3.25
☐ MG45657-1	#56 Keep Out, Claudia!	$3.25
☐ MG45658-X	#57 Dawn Saves the Planet	$3.25
☐ MG45659-8	#58 Stacey's Choice	$3.25
☐ MG45660-1	#59 Mallory Hates Boys (and Gym)	$3.25
☐ MG45662-8	#60 Mary Anne's Makeover	$3.50
☐ MG45663-6	#61 Jessi's and the Awful Secret	$3.50
☐ MG45664-4	#62 Kristy and the Worst Kid Ever	$3.50
☐ MG45665-2	#63 Claudia's Friend Friend	$3.50
☐ MG45666-0	#64 Dawn's Family Feud	$3.50
☐ MG45667-9	#65 Stacey's Big Crush	$3.50
☐ MG45575-3	Logan's Story Special Edition Readers' Request	$3.25
☐ MG44240-6	Baby-sitters on Board! Super Special #1	$3.95
☐ MG44239-2	Baby-sitters' Summer Vacation Super Special #2	$3.95
☐ MG43973-1	Baby-sitters' Winter Vacation Super Special #3	$3.95
☐ MG42493-9	Baby-sitters' Island Adventure Super Special #4	$3.95
☐ MG43575-2	California Girls! Super Special #5	$3.95
☐ MG43576-0	New York, New York! Super Special #6	$3.95
☐ MG44963-X	Snowbound Super Special #7	$3.95
☐ MG44962-X	Baby-sitters at Shadow Lake Super Special #8	$3.95
☐ MG45661-X	Starring the Baby-sitters Club Super Special #9	$3.95

Available wherever you buy books...or use this order form.

Scholastic Inc., P.O. Box 7502, 2931 E. McCarty Street, Jefferson City, MO 65102

Please send me the books I have checked above. I am enclosing $———
(please add $2.00 to cover shipping and handling). Send check or money order - no
cash or C.O.D.s please.

Name ————————————————————————————

Address ————————————————————————————

City———————————— State/Zip ————————————
Please allow four to six weeks for delivery. Offer good in the U.S. only. Sorry, mail orders are not
available to residents of Canada. Prices subject to change.